"...THE NEXT JACK REACHER!"

1

Indie rose from bed a little after six, as she usually did, kissed Sam on the lips as he slept and went into the bathroom to shower. When she came out a half hour later and dressed, she kissed him again, but this time she made sure he didn't sleep through it.

"Hey, Sleepyhead," she said. "The honeymoon's over, and it's time to get up and go back to real life. You've got rehearsal this afternoon, remember?"

"You go to rehearsal for me," Sam mumbled, "and I'll stay here and take care of Kenzie."

Her eyes went wide. "As tempting as that sounds, I can't sing like you can, so get your butt outta that bed, Mister! Come on, get up. I'm making eggs and sausage and hash browns this morning!" She said that last in a singsong voice, and Sam finally rolled over onto his back.

"Fine," he said. "For hash browns, I'll get up." He went through his morning stretching ritual, working the cramps out of his bad leg, and by the time he actually got up and went to the shower, Indie was cracking eggs into a bowl, and Kenzie was on a stool beside her, ready to whisk them all together.

Fifteen minutes later, Sam was in his chair and Kenzie bowed her head to say grace over their breakfast. When she had done so, Sam and Indie said, "Amen!" with her, and then it was time for the day to begin.

"Kenzie, stop tossing eggs under the table to Samson," Indie said, "he eats kitty food, not people food!"

"Sorry, Mommy," Kenzie said, but the little grin she was trying to hide told Sam that she wasn't really all that sorry. The cat was her pet and her responsibility, and she took him seriously on both counts; that meant feeding him, but feeding him stuff he liked, and he loved eggs!

"So what all are you girls up to today?" Sam asked.

"Well, we're going grocery shopping," Indie said. "Anything that wasn't frozen or canned went bad while we were gone, so I gotta replace a lot. And then we're going over to the preschool and get a certain Miss Kenzie registered, because it starts in two weeks, and she's all excited about it!"

"Yeah!" Kenzie said. "When you go to school, you get to make friends, and you get to eat lunches from

bags, and learn how to read and write and all kinds of stuff!"

Sam looked at her with his eyes wide. "Really?" he asked. "You get to do all that at school? I think I wanna go to school with Kenzie—that sounds more fun than workin'!"

Indie laughed, and so did Kenzie. "You can't go to school, it's not for old people, just for kids!"

This was the way their mornings went, when they were all at home where they belonged. Sam was glad to be there, and thoughts of how close he had come to never seeing his home or family again ran through his mind.

Sam and Indie had married only five weeks before, and immediately flew off to Hawaii for a luxurious honeymoon, but the next morning had been when the announcement came of the terrorist plot to try to blow up twelve cities with small suitcase nukes. Sam had seen something odd as they were flying out of Denver, and then again when they'd arrived at Honolulu, and when he put them together, he and Indie were able to track down one of the bombs.

When local Honolulu police were too swamped to pay attention to Sam's tips, he'd called Harry Winslow, an undercover operative of the Department of Homeland Security that Sam had helped out once before. Harry not only listened, he ended up recruiting Sam to track down the terrorist cell in Denver that had

actually initiated the entire plot. Their honeymoon already ruined, and with Kenzie in the care of their mothers in a cabin Sam had inherited from his father, they agreed to fly home and do what they could.

Sam found the terror cell, but a single error in judgment by Sam ended up costing the life of his friend and former police partner, Dan Jacobs, and then Sam was off across the country, chasing a lone fanatical terrorist who had concocted a plot to use one of the bombs to destroy a quarter of the country.

The plan was to set it off in Lake Mead, where it would contaminate the water that supplied seven states. If he had succeeded, it would have meant that millions of people would have had to relocate to other parts of the country to survive, while several million more, those too poor to move, would have died of radiation poisoning within months.

It was Indie who discovered the depth of the plot, and gave Sam the clue he needed to head it off, but he was severely wounded by the terrorist in the process. Another agent of Homeland Security, assigned to assist him, had taken the terrorist out just as he was trying once more to kill Sam. The bomb was disarmed, the plot was foiled, and Sam slipped into a coma that was almost the end of his life.

Sam Prichard wasn't one to go easily into that famous good night, however; defying the doctor's prediction of his demise, he had slowly gotten better, and wakened at

last to find his beloved Indie there beside the bed, tears streaking her face as she prayed for him to come back to her. Those prayers were answered, and Sam was able to leave the hospital only a few days later.

Harry had surprised them with a new honeymoon package, and they had just gotten back from it the day before. Kenzie had stayed with her grandmothers again, having the time of her life since both of them loved spoiling the child rotten. But now they were home, and Indie was right—it was time to get back to life. They had found a few calls on their voicemail, clients interested in hiring Sam for various investigative work, and several messages from Chris Lancaster, the lead guitarist and manager of the band that Sam sang with, demanding that he get to rehearsal as soon as possible, and bring them some new songs to learn. He had called Chris the night before and promised to make rehearsal that afternoon at two.

Indie was loading the dishes into the dishwasher while Sam was running all of this through his mind, and when she finished she turned to him.

"So," she said, "are there going to be any new songs today that I haven't heard? You know, you promised to play some for me weeks ago, and I still haven't heard them."

Sam grinned. "I still haven't found that old CD, yet. You'll get to hear them all soon, though; Chris says we're going into the studio next week, so we've got to work

DAVID ARCHER

hard to get songs ready before then. If you get done with all your errands this morning, you can always come down and listen."

She smiled, and came over to him, slipping her arms around him and stretching up for a kiss. When he let her up for air, she said, "You can count on us being there. A band needs an audience, right? That's mine and Kenzie's job!"

Sam hugged her close, and Kenzie came over to get in on it, so he reached down and lifted her up to join them. She giggled as he made growly sounds at her, and squeezed his neck tight.

"Mmm," he said, "a guy could start to like this!"

"You'd better," Indie said, "'cause we're gonna keep it up forever!"

Sam let them go, and Indie had Kenzie go and get dressed so they could go and take care of shopping and school registration, while she went to their bedroom to change from nightgown to street clothes. Sam followed, and stood by the door and smiled as he watched.

"What?" Indie asked when she saw him looking her way.

Sam shook his head gently. "Just admiring the view, babe," he said. "Just admiring the view!"

She laughed, and said, "You're crazy, I don't even have makeup on, yet!"

"Babe," Sam said, "you don't need any. You're beautiful just the way you are!"

"Yeah, well, I'm very glad you think so, Mr. Prichard, but I don't go out without it!" She slid a pair of jeans up her legs and wiggled her way into them, glaring at Sam the whole time, then pulled a long-sleeved white top over her head, hooking her hands into her hair to pull it all out of the collar. "Aren't you supposed to be calling clients?" she asked as she went into the bathroom.

"I guess I can do that," he said with a grin, and turned to go out to his office. He sat at his desk, picked up a pen and hit the Play button on the voicemail machine.

"Mr. Prichard, my name is Jim Durban, and I'd be interested in talking to you about a matter of marital infidelity..." Sam deleted that one, and the machine went to the next.

"Hello, I'm looking for Mr. Prichard," said a woman's voice. *"My name is Juliette Connors, and I have a matter of some urgency to discuss, involving assets my soon to be ex-husband is hiding, and if you'd call me back, I'd appreciate it. My number is..."* Sam made a note of the number; Indie could knock that one out in her sleep, and it might be worth some serious money.

There were a couple more like the first one—Sam didn't do wife or husband trailing, just as a matter of principle—and he deleted those as well. He hit play on the next to last one.

"Mr. Prichard," said a man, *"I'd like to talk to you*

about finding my wife. She disappeared about three months ago, and I've got people trying to say I've done something with her, but I haven't. Her sister claims that my wife told her she was afraid I was going to kill her. Mr. Prichard, I never was a threat to her, not in any way, and I don't know why she left, or where she could have gone, or anything, but my lawyer says just the fact that no one can find her is making me look bad. I need help, please. My name is Albert Corning, and my number is..." Sam wrote it down. This man sounded like he might have a real problem that needed his help.

The last call was different, though. When Sam hit play, he heard a recorded voice say, "Hello. This call is from" and another voice said, "Carl Morris," followed by the first, recorded voice, saying, "who is an inmate at the county jail. To accept the call, press five. To decline the call and block all future calls from this inmate, press nine." The call had come in the day before they got home, and there were no more calls after it.

Sam thought about it for a moment, but he was pretty sure he didn't know any Carl Morris. Still, it could be someone to whom he'd been recommended, so he looked at the number it had come from and dialed it back. A bored deputy answered, "Detention Center."

"Hi," Sam said. "Can you tell me if you still have a Carl Morris in jail there?"

There was a moment of silence, and then Sam heard whispering on the other end. He furrowed his brow,

wondering what was going on, but suddenly a different voice came on the line.

"You're looking for Carl Morris?" it asked, gruffly.

"Yes. I'm Sam Prichard, private investigator, and he left a message on my phone a few days ago from the jail. I was calling to see if he's still there."

"Well, Sam Prichard," the voice said. "This is Sheriff's Detective Orville Kennedy. I happened to be here at the detention center right now, because I'm officially notifying Carl Morris that he's been indicted on three counts of murder this morning. Is he a client of yours?"

Sam let his eyebrows come back down off his hairline. "Not yet," he said, "but then I haven't had the chance to speak with him yet. Can he be given a message to call me back?"

Detective Kennedy made a sound that was a cross between a chuckle and a snort. "Yeah, I can do that. Word to the wise, though," he added. "If you agree to work for him, get your money up front, and quick. His assets may be frozen pretty soon. Morris was indicted this morning on three counts of first-degree murder in the axe-murder-style deaths of his wife and their two kids. Wife's family is already talking about filing wrongful death lawsuits, so he may not have any way to pay you before too long."

Sam's eyebrows went back up. "You sound like you've got a pretty solid case. Any possibility of his

9

innocence?"

That snorting laugh came again. "I was at the scene," Kennedy said. "We found Morris passed out cold on the floor, right next to the bodies, and there was blood everywhere. His prints were on the old hatchet he used as a weapon, some of them even bloody prints, 'cause the blood was splattered everywhere, all over the room and all over him. He reeked of cheap whiskey, and had Adivol in his system. You know what that is? Sleeping pills, but when it's mixed with alcohol, it can cause some pretty bizarre behavior. No sign of a drinking problem before this. We couldn't wake him up, so we took him to jail and let him sleep it off. When he woke up, he said he didn't have any idea how he got there, and didn't remember anything, so I told him what he'd done, and the guy just fell apart and flipped out. He's a big mother, a bodybuilder, and it took eight of us to restrain him and the nurse had to give him a shot to calm him down. You figure it out—I sure as hell can't."

Sam wrote down what he was hearing. "All right," he said. "Please, tell him to call me. You never know, he might have something to say, and if it seems appropriate, I'll call you."

"You do that," Kennedy said, and hung up.

Sam looked at the number for Albert Corning, the man who said his wife was missing, and dialed it. It rang twice, and then the same voice as the one on the message answered the phone.

"Hello?"

"Mr. Corning? This is Sam Prichard, private investigator. I'm returning your call."

"Yes!" Corning said excitedly. "Mr. Prichard, thanks for calling me back, I really appreciate it! This has turned into a nightmare!"

"Well, I heard what you left on my voicemail," Sam said. "Can you give me a bit more information?"

"Sure," Corning said. "About four months ago, my wife Annie started acting strangely, and I have no idea why. She started going out and being gone for hours without answering her phone, and a few times she took some money out of the bank but swore she didn't know where it went, and then I woke up in the middle of the night a few times to find her gone, but she'd come in sometime in the early hours of the next morning and say she just couldn't sleep and went for a drive. The next morning, she'd insist I dreamed the whole thing, that she hadn't gone anywhere. I asked her if she was seeing someone, having an affair, and she always swore she wasn't, and that everything was fine between us. Then, three months ago, I came home from work on a Tuesday and she was gone, but no one has seen her since then. She left her clothes, didn't take any extra money out of the bank; the only thing I can tell she took with her is her purse. Her car was found abandoned at Wal-Mart."

Sam pursed his lips. "Mr. Corning, did you ever find

any kind of evidence of an affair? Was she inattentive to you, did she seem cold or standoffish?"

"That's the thing," Corning said, "she always acted like everything was good! We made love almost every night, and she was always doing little things for me, like making me coffee and bringing it to me in the mornings, or getting herself all prettied up before I got home from work, meeting me at the door in a negligee—I thought she was just going through some kind of a phase, and I tried not to worry about it, you know? But then she just vanished, and I have tried everything I can think of to find her on my own, and now her kids and her sister are saying I killed her or something! I can't sleep, I can't work, I can't even think! I need help, Mr. Prichard."

Sam nodded into the phone. "Yeah, it sounds like it. Listen, can you come over to my office this morning? Say in a half hour?" Corning agreed, and Sam gave him the address.

He hung up the phone and looked at the other number he'd made a note of: Juliette Connors. He dialed the number and it was answered on the first ring.

"Hello?" he heard, in a low, sultry voice.

"Mrs. Connors? This is Sam Prichard, private eye, returning your call."

"Oh, yes, Mr. Prichard," she said. "I'm glad to hear back from you. I've got a problem, I'm afraid; my husband Alex and I are getting a divorce, and in the financial disclosures we both have to make, he's missing

some assets that I know exist. I'm looking for help in finding where he's hidden them. Is that something you can do? An old friend of mine suggested I call you, and said you'd know his name—Jimmy Smith?"

Sam stifled a groan. Jimmy Smith was a former client who had hired Sam to clear him of a murder charge that Sam had helped to bring against him. Sam had thought Smith would never want anything to do with him again, even though he'd been quite generous with his fee and bonus.

"Yes," Sam said, "I know Jimmy. And I think I can help you with your problem. Could you come by the office later this morning, say around ten-thirty?" Once again he gave out his address, and sat back to think about the strange cases he was looking at.

Mrs. Connors' case wasn't too bad. Sam was fairly sure that once he knew what assets were being hidden, Indie could track them down pretty quickly. Corning's case, on the other hand, could be a pickle. If his wife had vanished voluntarily then she was one of the "maliciously-missing" that police often complained about. These people were often very hard to track, especially if they'd done any research on how to disappear without a trace. In most cases, they didn't turn up until something almost coincidental happened, like running into someone they knew, or getting fingerprinted after some minor arrest.

On the other hand, if someone had orchestrated her

disappearance, then Sam could be looking for a body, and then a killer. If Corning was actually innocent, then there was someone out there who knew the truth, and Sam's job would be to figure out who that might be and bring them in for questioning.

He was letting all of this roll through his mind when his desk phone rang. He answered it, saying, "Sam Prichard, Private Eye."

"*Hello. This call is from*" and he heard Morris's voice say, "Carl Morris," and then the recording continued, "*who is an inmate at the county jail. To accept the call, press five. To decline the call and block all future calls from this inmate, press nine.*"

Sam punched the five, and then said, "Hello?"

"Mr. Prichard? This is Carl Morris. The detective said you wanted me to call you back?"

"Yes, Mr. Morris," Sam said. "I got your message and called this morning to see if they'd tell you to call me back, and ended up talking to Detective Kennedy. From what he told me, you're in quite a mess."

"Ha!" Morris said. "Yes, I guess you could say that. I've been charged with killing my wife and kids, and they just told me that they're going for the death penalty."

Sam sighed. This man's voice said that he had already given up, and a hopeless man wasn't the best to work with. "What did you want from me, Mr. Morris?"

Morris was quiet for a long moment, and then said, "Mr. Prichard, I suppose I'm hoping you can find out

just why I did it."

Sam's eyes went wide again. "Mr. Morris—you're saying you're guilty?"

"Mr. Prichard, here's what I know," Morris said. "I was found unconscious beside the bodies of my family on my living room floor. The doors were all locked from the inside, and the police had to break in. I was unconscious, like I said, and they couldn't rouse me, so they brought me here and did blood tests, and found that I was drunk and had drugs in my system, the kind of drugs that supposedly can make you do this sort of thing. When they told me what I'd done, I just lost it, and they had to sedate me, but I've come to grips with it now." He sighed. "The murder weapon was an old tomahawk that I've owned for more than twenty years, and it had my prints all over it, including many of them in my family's blood. Since there is no way anyone else could have done this, Mr. Prichard, what I want to know is how and why I did it. Y'see, Mr. Prichard, I don't ever drink, and I don't take any kind of drugs, not even aspirin. It's sort of a phobia, because I hear all the possible side effects on TV commercials, and I just can't see putting that stuff into my body. So I want to know how I got drunk, and how I had this sleeping drug in me, since that combination is probably what made me do this. And then I want to know what could have triggered me doing something like this."

The longer Sam had listened to Morris, the more he was getting an eerie feeling that something about this case

wasn't right. "Mr. Morris, if you want to hire me, then I need to come down and see you. I can be there around noon, if that's okay with you."

"I'd like that very much, Mr. Prichard. Shall I tell them you'll be coming?"

"Yes, do," Sam said. "They know me down there, it won't be a problem."

Sam got off the phone and read through the notes he'd made several times. If Morris was telling the truth, then Sam couldn't help but wonder how any combination of drugs and alcohol could bring something like that out of a man who wasn't already prone to violence. He made a note to ask Morris about his mental health history, and to have Indie find anything she could on the man and his family. If he had any kind of a record, she'd find it, and it might tell Sam something about how this might have happened.

Meanwhile, he wasn't entirely computer illiterate himself. He went to the local newspaper's website and ran a search for Morris's name, and found the stories that had run already.

"Aurora Family Slain In Grisly Triple Murder," screamed the first headline. The story underneath it told how police had received a tip that Carl Morris, thirty-four years old, had murdered his wife (Genevieve, thirty-three) and children (David, sixteen, and Elana, thirteen) by hacking them to pieces with an old Indian tomahawk. They had arrived to find the house locked up tight from

the inside, and when they'd seen through a window what appeared to be bodies, they had broken in to find the three victims, and Carl unconscious on the floor beside their bodies.

Carl was taken to the jail, where blood tests were run; he was found to have alcohol and zolpidem, a drug most commonly sold under the brand name Adivol, in his system. Zolpidem, the article said, is known to have side effects that can include hallucinations, especially when taken with alcohol, and there was speculation that this may have played a part in the horrific crime.

Neighbors said they were shocked, and that Morris had never seemed to have any sort of drinking problem. Most described the family as happy and always friendly, and it was noted that they'd had a big cookout at their house only two nights earlier, with most of the block in attendance.

Sam read several of the articles that were available online, and found the same things in all of them. Police got a tip, went to the house and found Morris out cold on the floor beside the bodies. The house was locked from the inside, and there was no sign of any other person having been present at the time of the killings. Despite the odd things about the case, such as the anonymous tip—who else could have known about the crime was still a mystery—police said the preponderance of the evidence led to Carl as the perpetrator, regardless of how nice a guy his neighbors thought he was.

The only person who seemed to believe that Carl was innocent was a teenaged girl who had been a friend of his children. Her name was Miranda Nielsen, and she insisted that she knew the family well and could never believe that Morris would harm his wife and kids.

The whole thing was so screwy that Sam couldn't imagine how it could have happened. Without knowing more about Morris, he was at a standstill. He picked up his phone to call his old partner on the force, Dan Jacobs, to ask him to run Morris' background.

He put down the phone. Danny was dead, and for just a moment, he'd forgotten. Danny was dead, and Sam would never quite be able to forgive himself for the lapse in judgment that had led to his death.

He got up and went into the house to get himself a cup of coffee; thinking about Danny wouldn't help, and he knew it wasn't really his fault, but he also knew he'd go through this from time to time. He'd cope with it; if Sam was anything, he was a survivor, and guilt was something you had to learn to live with.

He went back to his office and sat there making notes until Corning arrived.

2

"Mr. Corning," Sam said as he opened the office door for him. "Come on in and have a seat." He extended a hand, and Corning shook it firmly.

"Thanks for seeing me," Corning said as he sat down in the chair in front of Sam's desk. "I'm about at my wits' end, and when you didn't call back right away, I tried other investigators, but none of them wanted to talk to me about this."

"Missing persons are always tough cases," Sam said. "I was out on my honeymoon when you called, and just got your message this morning, I'm afraid."

"Well, in that case, congratulations, and thanks for getting back to me so quickly! How do we start this?"

Sam turned on his recorder, but also picked up a pen to make notes. "First thing we do is, you tell me everything you know about the situation. Let's start with

some background on you and your wife."

Corning nodded. "Okay," he said. "Well, I'm Albert James Corning, I was born August fourth, nineteen seventy-nine, right here in Denver. Joined the Army at eighteen, spent four years in as a medic, got out in oh-three and went to work as an EMT with the fire department, been there ever since. I've made some good investments, and my net worth is about eight hundred thousand. Never been in any kind of trouble, other than a few traffic tickets over the years. I think the last one was back in oh-nine."

He paused and leaned his head back for a moment, then went on. "My wife is Annie Leanne Mitchell Corning, born January sixth, nineteen eighty-two, in Aurora. I met Annie right after I started at the department; she was working in dispatch, and we started dating. Got married after dating a year, and we've never had any real problems. She got restless back in oh-six, after we found out she couldn't have kids, and went to stay with her sister for a month, but came back home after that and we've been great ever since. We looked at adoption, but after a while she decided she just wanted to spend time in charity work, so she's been a volunteer with a bunch of them over the years. Her favorite was always working with the troubled kids at the Mary Williams Foundation in Aurora."

Sam held up a hand to stop him. "Do you know who she worked with at these places, especially the ones she's been working at lately?"

Corning nodded. "The last two years, she's only worked at Mary Williams and twice a month at the homeless shelter over on Tenth Street, on their food line. That was every other Sunday, and the guy who runs it is Pastor Evans from the Tenth Street Baptist Church. I know him, he's a pretty nice guy. Mary Williams is run by a woman named Charlotte Peters, but there's a lot of people working there, some on payroll and some volunteers like Annie. The only one she ever spent any of her free time with was a woman named Cindy Benton; they got to be friends when they had to deal with this one girl who was always getting into trouble."

Sam nodded. "Okay. What about Annie's background? Any troubles in her past?"

Corning looked down and to the left, which Sam knew meant that he was thinking of how to answer, and whether to answer truthfully. After a second, he looked up and said, "This isn't something I'd want getting out, of course, but a couple years before we met, Annie was involved in some things that she isn't very proud of. A boyfriend of hers had gotten her to do some porn movies, said it was just private stuff, but a few years ago, they turned up on the Internet. Someone tracked her down and it was pretty embarrassing. They tried to shake us down for money, but we talked it over and refused to pay. Annie even went forward at our church and admitted to it, and the people were great about it, let her know that the mistakes we made in the past don't matter, once we accept Christ." He ran his hands over his face.

"Other than that, there's been nothing, not until she started acting strange."

"Okay," Sam said, "now let's talk about that. What was the first thing you noticed?"

Corning thought for a moment, and said, "She stopped answering her cell phone. I'd always call or text her during the day, and she used to always answer or respond, but suddenly she just stopped. That was about four months ago, and I asked her why, and she'd say the phone never rang, or she just was too busy to answer, or she got distracted and forgot to answer a text. Seemed like most of the time when I'd call her, she didn't answer. Sometimes she would, but even then, it was like she wanted to get off the phone in a hurry."

Sam made a note. "And then?"

"Well, about two weeks after she started acting weird, I woke up and she was gone, about 1 a.m.. I tried calling but her phone was on the nightstand, and she came back about four. I was pretty upset, and I guess I yelled a little, but she swore she just couldn't sleep and went for a drive. That happened about four or five times before she left. Then I came home one day, it was a Tuesday, I remember, and she wasn't home. I tried calling, but she didn't answer, like usual, so I just made dinner and waited, but she never came home. I tried filing a missing person report, but the cops wouldn't take one till she'd been gone forty-eight hours, and then they found her car in the parking lot at a Wal-Mart in Aurora, but there's

been no other trace of her since then." He ran his hands over his face again.

Sam said, "Mr. Corning..."

"Al, please," Corning said. "Everyone calls me Al."

"Okay, Al—on the message you left, you said Annie's sister is saying that your wife said she was afraid of you?"

Corning nodded. "Yeah, she came forward about two weeks after Annie vanished and said Annie told her she was afraid I was going to kill her, but never said why. Her name is Connie, Connie Dozier. She's married to Ron Dozier, the lawyer, and they've managed to get the police to open an investigation into whether I did something to my wife, but I swear I didn't. I hired a lawyer myself, Carol Spencer; she says the cops could try to charge me with murder, even though they don't have a body."

Sam nodded. "If they have enough circumstantial evidence, it's possible, but I doubt it's likely unless they get something that they can consider physical evidence. Have they searched your home?"

Corning rolled his eyes. "Five times, so far," he said. "They took my car and Annie's and went through them, and they say they haven't found anything to support the idea that I've done anything to her, but they won't stop pushing. They've called me in for questioning a dozen times, and the only thing they say is that my story seems to be the same every time. It's like they want to make me say something else, so they can charge me with

something!"

"Yeah, cops can be pretty brutal, but that's their job. If you did do something, they're supposed to find out and bring you to justice, but it does seem like they're going after you harder than usual. Is there anything else you can tell me that might explain that?"

Corning shrugged. "Not that I can think of," he said. "Everyone down at Mary Williams is still supportive; they say she never led them to think there was any problem, or that she was afraid of me. Pastor Evans just says they miss her, but he won't really talk to me. I'm just praying she's okay somewhere, and that she'll come home, but I don't know what to think. That's why I need help, Mr. Prichard."

Sam smiled. "That's what I'm here for," he said, "and you can call me Sam. Al, I get a thousand dollar retainer, and I charge two fifty a day plus expenses. If that's okay with you, I'll get started right away."

Corning nodded, and took out his wallet. "I anticipated as much, and brought cash." He counted out ten one hundred dollar bills onto Sam's desk, and then handed over a photo of him and his wife. "I hope you can find her, Sam." He shook Sam's hand again, then stood and left without another word.

Sam sat there and went through his notes, deciding to talk to the Pastor first. He Googled his phone number and dialed.

"Pastor Evans? My name is Sam Prichard, and I'm a

private investigator. I've been hired by Albert Corning to look into the disappearance of his wife, and wondered if you might have any information that could help."

The minister was quiet for a moment. "Mr. Prichard, Mrs. Corning is a very troubled woman. I don't know much about their home life, but she was always talking about how there were things she couldn't say to her husband, and sometimes she would confide in me, but I can't say there was ever anything that could explain her disappearing like this. I'll confess that I've wondered if something has happened to her, but I can't say there's any particular thing that makes me think so. I've told all this to the police, of course."

"When she confided in you, Pastor, was it ever about any kind of extramarital affair? She seems to have been acting strangely before she left."

"Oh, no," the pastor said hastily. "I don't think that was ever an issue with them. In fact, she told me often that they were extremely happy together, but that there were certain things she couldn't talk to him about."

"Do you know what sort of things she might have meant? Pastor, I know there's some confidentiality in her conversations with you, but anything you can tell me might help."

The minister sighed. "She was concerned that her husband was working too hard, that was one thing, but said he wouldn't listen when she brought it up. He's an EMT, you know, and I guess he takes his work very

seriously. The only other thing she said was that he didn't ever want to talk about the past, and sometimes she wanted to get closure on things. I'm afraid she never told me what they were."

Sam wrote what he had heard and thanked him for his time. He was thinking of calling Charlotte Peters at the Mary Williams home when he heard a car pull up in the driveway. Juliette Connors was arriving twenty minutes early, and Sam got up to let her in.

"Hi, Mr. Prichard?" she said as he opened the door. "I hope you don't mind I'm a little early, I wasn't sure where you were, so I wanted to make sure I wasn't late."

"No problem," Sam said, shaking her hand. "Please come in and have a seat." He led her to the same chair Corning had vacated only a few minutes before. She sat down, and it suddenly hit Sam that she was wearing an awfully short skirt, and her top was cut almost low enough to be illegal in some states. This was a woman who thought her looks would get her anything she wanted, he knew, but all Sam was interested in was the money he could make from helping her find whatever assets her husband was trying to hide. That sort of case got a percentage, and if the assets were truly valuable, the reward could be pretty good.

"Now," he said, keeping his eyes firmly glued to hers, "I got the gist of your problem. If you can give me some of the specifics, we'll see how I can help."

She rolled her eyes. "Where to start?" she said.

"Well, my husband Alex and I are getting divorced, and we're each supposed to divulge our assets, so the court can divide them equitably. Alex is a dentist, and he's done quite well while we were married, investing a lot of money into stocks that have really soared in value. Now, though, his money seems to be all hidden somewhere, and he's come up with business records claiming he's had a lot of losses in the past couple of years. I know he's got at least thirty million hidden away, and legally, half of that is mine, since he had nothing when we got married. Besides, it was me that worked and paid his way through dental school, and that's where he got the money he invested. What I want to know is how he hid the money, and where, so the court can divide it fairly and I get my share."

Sam nodded, smiling at how quickly she'd spoken. "Do you have any idea how he's hiding it? I mean, hasn't he paid taxes on the money? There has to be some kind of records."

She leaned forward, showing a lot of cleavage. "See, that's the thing," she said. "Alex is a tax protester, so he's always reinvesting his earnings, deferring the taxes and then making sure his top investments are offshore, through foreign investment companies. He's got it in his head that, by doing it this way, the IRS can't find his money and make him pay, but I think he's just courting disaster. If there's one thing about the IRS, it's that they never give up! If you've got it, they'll find it, and I want to find it before they do and get mine!"

Sam made a note. "Well, to be honest, I'm fairly sure I can find anything he's got hidden. I'll need a lot of information, like his social security number, date of birth, and all of his email and social media accounts."

She smiled and took an envelope from her purse. "I had my attorney draft this up," she said. "It's all of that information and a whole lot more."

Sam grinned as he took it and skimmed the documents inside. "This looks pretty complete," he said. "I get a retainer of one thousand dollars, and in a case like this, I take ten percent of any recovered assets."

She smiled. "That sounds fair enough, since my lawyers will make him pay the fees, anyway, once we prove he's been hiding assets." She took out a checkbook and wrote him a check for a thousand dollars without batting an eye. "I'll look forward to hearing from you," she said as she handed it over, and he showed her out a moment later, just as Indie pulled into the driveway in their truck. He stepped out and introduced Indie to Mrs. Connors, and gave her a short account of the case he'd just taken. Indie smiled, knowing that this one would likely be hers.

Since he was already outside, he helped Indie carry in the groceries she'd bought, and told her about Albert Corning and Carl Morris, as well.

"Wow," she said. "You've had an exciting morning, especially with Mrs. Come-and-get-it, there. If that skirt was any shorter, she'd be arrested for indecent

exposure!"

Sam laughed. "Some women think they get what they want by being flirtatious. That doesn't work on me."

Indie glared at him for a moment, then relaxed. "I know it doesn't," she said. "I tried flirting with you that first week I was here, and you didn't even notice!"

"Oh, I noticed," he said with a grin, "but I had promised not to make a pass, so I pretended you weren't getting to me. If I'd known how well things were gonna work out, I might have noticed better and let you seduce me!"

Indie threw a bag of beans at him, and he caught it, laughing, then dropped it onto the counter and spun to throw both arms around his wife. He kissed her, and she let out a low moan, then pushed him away. "Stop it," she said. "If you've got to be at the jail at noon, I need to make an early lunch. How about grilled cheese and tomato soup?"

"Sounds like a winner to me," Sam said.

"Cool, and easy. I got Kenzie all registered, by the way. She starts in two weeks!"

Kenzie came running into the kitchen just then, with Samson in hot pursuit. The cat was running, which was always comical, since he'd suffered nerve damage from a bout of distemper as a kitten, and his back legs suddenly came around in front and he went tumbling across the floor. He rolled to a stop, then shook his head and got up, walking sedately to where Kenzie had also come to a

stop. He contented himself with licking her legs as she looked up at Sam.

"Daddy," Kenzie said, "Mommy said we get to go hear you sing today."

Sam reached down and picked her up, causing the cat to stumble when the leg he was leaning on suddenly rose into the air. "That's right, Sweetie. You like that, don't you?"

"Yeah," she said, "cause Stan keeps M&M's for me!" Stan was the band's drummer, and they rehearsed in his big garage.

"Hmm," Indie said. "I'm gonna have to have a talk with Stan!"

Kenzie looked at her, panic stricken. "But, Mommy, M&M's are good!"

"Yes, they are, and they're full of sugar! Stan doesn't pay your dental bills, we do!"

Sam decided it was time to derail a potential argument. "Hey, Kenzie, we're gonna have grilled cheese and tomato soup for lunch! Think Samson will like that?"

Indie grabbed his face with both hands. "Samson," she said through clenched teeth, "eats *kitty food* for lunch!" She kissed him then, and let go, turning to the refrigerator to get out the cheese and start making their lunch, while Sam and Kenzie sat down and took turns holding Samson in their laps.

When lunch was over, Sam took Indie aside and

asked her to start looking into everything she could find on Carl Morris, and to call him if she found anything that stood out and might shed any light on his case. A moment later, he got into his Corvette and drove down to the detention center. The jailer saw him come in and said, "Prichard, right? I got a note you'd be coming down to see Carl Morris. Have a seat and we'll get it set up for you."

"Thanks," Sam said, and took a seat in one of the plastic chairs along the wall. A moment later, a female jailer came to get him.

"Mr. Prichard? If you'll follow me, please?" Sam got up and followed her down a hallway to the interview room he'd been in before with Jimmy Smith. "You're seeing Mr. Morris?" she asked, and Sam nodded.

"Yeah," he said. "He wants to talk about how I might be able to find out why he killed his family."

The jailer nodded. "He's kind of an enigma," she said. "He's probably one of the nicest men we've ever seen here, but what he did—it's just terrible. Though, some of us wonder if he's been framed; he just doesn't seem the type, you know what I mean?"

Sam nodded again. "I know exactly what you mean, and I can say there are things about the case that bother me. I'm hoping he can clear some of them up for me."

She led him into the interview room, and left him alone there. It was about five minutes later when Morris was escorted into the room by another jailer, a man, and

handcuffed to the table. The jailer left and closed the door behind him.

Sam looked Morris over. The man was not terribly tall, standing about five nine, but he was quite muscular, and it was apparent that he must work out regularly. His face was broad and serene, the face of a man who was comfortable with who he was and not worried about what others might think.

"Mr. Prichard," he said. "Thank you for coming. I know that this sort of a case is hard for anyone to deal with, but I can assure you that you can't possibly think worse of me than I think of myself."

Sam looked at him for another moment before replying. "Mr. Morris, at this point, I'm not sure what I think. I did some research on your case, and frankly, there are things about it that bother me. Apparently someone knew that your family was dead and tipped the police. Do you have any idea who it could have been?"

Morris shook his head. "The police have asked me that a dozen times," he said, "but I have no idea. It's the one thing I wish I knew, because that person may know what really happened that night. I just want to know how and why I could have done this. They're saying they want to go for the death penalty, and I don't blame them, but I'd like to know the answers to those questions before I go into that room for the injections. Then I could go to my Maker in peace, I think."

Sam cocked his head. "You sound like you're certain

that you did this, Carl. Have you considered the possibility that you may have been framed?"

Morris looked down at the tabletop. "I've had thoughts like that," he said, "but I cast them out when they come. I couldn't bear to let myself believe that, and then find out that I really did do it. It's better to just accept the responsibility and deal with that, I think."

"Carl, the police say someone tipped them off that they'd find your family dead in that house, even though it was locked from the inside. I don't know yet where that tip came from, but it seems to me that there is at least a chance that you were drugged, your family was murdered, and then you were put into place to look like you did it."

"My prints, my bloody prints, were on the tomahawk," Morris said. "I had my wife's and children's blood on my hands while I was holding it, while I was hacking them to death with it."

Sam shrugged. "It's possible that you didn't. Your hand could have been smeared in their blood after they were dead, and then wrapped around the handle, so that it would leave your prints there, and..."

"Mr. Prichard, I don't want to hear theories about how it might have happened, how I might be innocent. I was the one there, and there's nothing to suggest anyone else did this. What I want you to do, sir, is find out how I ended up drunk and drugged. If someone did that to me, then maybe some of the guilt is not mine, but as far

as the police are concerned, and as far as I'm concerned, I am the one who held that tomahawk and killed my family with it. Now, if you'll do that for me, then I will be happy to pay whatever you want."

Morris was looking Sam in the eye, and the feeling that went through him was eerie. It was as if Morris wanted to be guilty of this heinous crime, but wanted someone else to be responsible for that guilt. Sam had never seen such a thing before, and it spooked him.

"Very well," he said. "Then that's what I'll do."

Morris smiled. "Thank you," he said. "If you'll go to see my attorney, Carol Spencer, she'll pay your retainer and fees. Please let me know about anything you find, as soon as you are able." He lowered his eyes to the table once more.

"Before we get to that," Sam said, "tell me about the last couple of days before the murders. What was going on in your family that last couple of days?"

Morris looked him in the eye again. "Not much, nothing out of the ordinary. We had a party a couple nights earlier, had most of the neighbors over, and after that everything was normal. I went to work, my wife went to her job, the kids did whatever they do. The night it happened, I came home like always and Elana, my daughter, asked me to help her move her bedroom furniture around, so we did that, and then I went down to watch some TV with my wife. I don't remember drinking anything at all, but the next thing I knew, I woke

up in the hospital, chained to the bed, and there were four cops standing guard over me. They told me what had happened, and I sort of lost it, and then that detective came in and made me look at pictures they took before they even moved me. There I was, covered in their blood." He suddenly had tears streaming down his face. "Mr. Prichard, I had their blood all over me, even on my face. It was on my lips, as if I'd been kissing them while I was killing them. What kind of monster does this kind of thing?"

Sam shook his head. "I don't know the answer to that, Carl," he said, "but I can promise you I'm gonna find out. I'll let you know what I learn as I learn it. Call me whenever you need to, and especially if you remember anything that you think will help."

Sam knocked for the jailer, and the man came to take Morris back to his cell. A moment later, the woman returned to escort Sam out of the secure areas of the detention center.

"See what I mean?" she asked. "When you talk to him, you just can't quite believe he did this, can you?"

Sam shrugged his shoulders. "You just don't know what people can do, sometimes," he said, "but in this case, I have to agree. Something just doesn't fit, and I'm gonna do my best to find out what it is."

She looked at him. "We're afraid he's going to hurt himself. He's on suicide watch, already, because they always put people who kill loved ones on it, but

35

somehow I don't think that would stop him."

Sam looked at her and smiled sadly. "He won't," he said, "not until he knows the answers to his questions." He nodded once more and left the building.

When he got to his car, it was only twelve-thirty, so he called Indie to let her know he was coming home and could ride with her and Kenzie to rehearsal.

"Good," she said. "I want to show you something about Carl Morris, anyway, and I don't want to talk about it on the phone."

"Okay, babe, I'll be there in twenty minutes." He started the car and pushed it a bit to get there on time.

3

"I was able to find a couple of things about Carl Morris that are interesting, but I'm not sure they're related," Indie said when Sam got home. "I tracked down his Facebook, and from that he seems like a pretty normal guy, so I looked at his friends list, and check this out." She clicked on a link and another Facebook profile popped up. "Look familiar?" Indie asked, and Sam let out a low whistle. The profile that came up was for Jimmy Smith, the talent agent who had been framed for murder a few weeks earlier.

"That's curious," Sam said. "Probably not related, but we'll check it out. And it's doubly curious because Juliette Connors said Jimmy recommended me to her. I wonder if he told Carl to get hold of me, too."

"No way to tell, from this, but you might want to ask him the next time you talk to him. I mean, if Jimmy's

sending you business, that's cool."

"True. You said you found a couple of things, so what else was there?"

She did a half shrug. "Well, everyone says he's Mister Mellow, but Carl Morris has a history of violence. Back in ninety-seven, he was arrested for beating a man severely in an argument at a gym, charged with 'assault with a deadly weapon.' The deadly weapon in this case was his hands! He got probation, went to anger management, and hasn't been in any trouble since then, but I thought you should know about it. Other than that, I can't even find a rumor of any problem around him. Pillar of the community type, he is."

Sam nodded. "So I see. Even the jailers think he must have been framed, and frankly, I'm halfway leaning that direction already. The only ones who really think he did are the cops and himself, but it just bugs me that someone tipped the police and had to have known about it, but they aren't even taking that into consideration."

Indie shrugged. "They might be," she said. "Just because it isn't in the newspapers doesn't mean they aren't looking into it. Is there anyone you can call and ask?"

Sam looked sad, suddenly, and Indie regretted her question, but then he said, "I can try the detective in charge of the case—he's with the sheriff's office. I'll give him a quick call, and then we've got to head for rehearsals." He took out his phone and called the

sheriff's office, asking for Detective Kennedy. He was put through almost instantly.

"Kennedy," the man answered.

"Detective Kennedy, this is Sam Prichard," he said. "If you've got a minute, I'd like to ask you a couple of things about the Carl Morris case."

Kennedy sighed. "Somehow I just knew I was gonna be talking to you again soon, Sam Prichard. What do you need?"

"Well, I've talked to Carl and been hired, but he's not asking me to prove he didn't do it—he wants me to find out how he got the alcohol and drugs in his system, because he thinks that's what made him do this."

"Yeah, I know," Kennedy said. "Sad thing when a man does something like this, isn't it?"

"Yeah, it is, but there are a few things bothering me. From what I've read and been told, someone called in an anonymous tip the night his family was killed, telling you guys what you'd find there. Do you have any idea who it was, and if not, are you doing anything to try to find out?"

"Well, we don't know who it was, no, and the reason we get anonymous tips is because they come in on an anonymous tip line. That line doesn't record the numbers of incoming calls. That's why people are willing to call in on it. As for trying to find out who it is, of course we are. Whoever it was had knowledge of a felony, and failing to come forward and provide further

information they might have is a felony in itself." He sighed. "Now, if what you're really asking is whether we've considered the possibility that whoever made that tip may have been the actual perpetrator, the answer is a very precise 'maybe,' and I say that off the record, got that? There's things about this case that are bothering me, too, like the fact that there is no trace of Adivol in that house, anywhere, not in Morris's car, or anywhere else associated with him. You'd think that if he were taking it at all, there'd be some more around someplace, right? I would, and since I know that you're an ex-vice cop, I know you're thinking that's strange, same way I do. And by the way—sorry about Dan Jacobs. I know he was your partner, and even if you're not on the force anymore, I know it hurts."

Sam swallowed. "Thanks," he said, "and yeah, that strikes me as odd, too. What else is bothering you?"

Kennedy seemed to lean closer to the phone and speak more softly. "Okay, again, this is off the record, but you may be able to do something with it that I can't. Morris was being stalked by a woman, and he'd tried to get her to leave him alone without involving police, because she was married and he didn't want to ruin her life. She was following him around, even showing up at his house in the middle of the night and trying to get him to come out and talk to her. I only know about this because he'd confided in one of the neighbors, but he told me about it when I asked. The funny thing is, it all came to a sudden stop a few months ago, and when I got

to digging, I found out that the reason it stopped is because the woman who was stalking him disappeared, herself. Denver PD is running the investigation, but they seem to think her husband did her in and got rid of the body."

Sam's blood ran cold. "Don't tell me—Annie Corning?"

Kennedy sounded surprised that Sam knew the name. "How did you know that? Did he tell you?"

"No," Sam said. "But her husband hired me this morning to try to find out what happened to her."

"Well, you don't need to look at Morris for that one," Kennedy said. "I checked it out thoroughly, and the day she disappeared, he wasn't even in town, he was in a bodybuilding competition in California in front of thirty thousand people. He couldn't have had anything to do with it."

"Okay," Sam said. "Anything else you can tell me? Like, what was the actual tip message, can you tell me that?"

Kennedy was quiet for a moment, but Sam could hear papers rustling. "Here it is," Kennedy said. "It said, 'Some people are being murdered at sixty-four ninety-two West Garvin Court in Aurora.' That was all. The voice was garbled, like it was run through a computer, but our tech guys think it was a male voice. They're trying to unscramble it, but they say they don't know if they'll be able to or not." He fell silent for a moment,

then said, "There is one more thing. There's a girl, a teenager who hung out at their house a lot. We think she had a crush on Morris, but I don't think that's related. The thing is, she says there was no possible way Morris would ever hurt anyone, that she knows because she'd seen him deal with some serious stuff, and he never, ever lost his cool. When I asked her what kinds of things, she got evasive, but said that one of them was when he found out his wife had been having an affair a year or so back. All he did was ask her to give him another chance to be a better husband, and they'd been doing great since then, I guess. I know she's just a kid, but I have to agree with her that a man like that doesn't sound like a killer."

Sam nodded into the phone, and said, "Yeah, I agree. Something about this just isn't adding up. Listen, thanks for talking to me, and if I do get anything, I'll return the favor as soon as I can." He ended the call as Indie came walking up to him.

"Get anything?" she asked, but Sam just shook his head.

"A lot," he said, "but we'll talk about it later. For now, let's go make some music and I'll let it all roll around back in that black hole I call my mind."

"Sounds good," she said, and then she kissed him. "I love it when you sing, you know."

"Good, cause I'm singing for you! Other people can listen if they want, I don't care, but I'm singing for you, babe!"

They finished getting ready, made sure Samson wasn't getting out of the house, and climbed into the truck to go to Stan's place. It was about a forty minute drive through city traffic, and they got there a little early. The band was all there, though, and Candy and Janice were delighted to see them after they'd been away for so long. None of them knew the details of Sam's involvement in stopping the terrorist attack, and had been told that Sam was wounded while stopping a robbery he'd stumbled upon. They all let him know how glad they were that they weren't looking for yet another new lead singer.

"Okay," Chris said, while Stan was showing Kenzie where the new bag of M&M's was hidden, "we're opening at the Casino this weekend, debuting our new full country show. Sam, I hope you've got some songs ready, Buddy."

Sam grinned. "I do," he said, "I just hope you guys can stand them. These are some of the ones we used to do when I was in college, but I've dressed 'em up a little. I think I'm a better songwriter now than I was back then, anyway."

"Just let us have 'em, man," Chris said. "We'll make you sound good, don't you worry!"

"Okay, well, somebody gimme a guitar, and we'll see." Stan handed him an acoustic, and Sam settled onto the stool they kept there for him because of his bad hip. "This one was always fun. It starts off with a riff from

Elvis's big comeback show, you know, da-da-*dah,* da-da-*duh,* da-da-*dah,* da-da-*duh.* Then we go into a thumping beat. It goes like this."

He began to play, and Chris joined in instantly, following along. Stan was next with the drums, then Candy and Janice caught up. They ran through the melody once, and then Sam said, "You got it, now let's do it!"

Woke up this mornin' and the sun was shinin' in, and I just knew the day was gonna be a good'un!

Kicked off all the covers, started getting' outta bed, when I heard a voice say "Boy, I wish you would'n',"

So I looked around the room, it was just as I had thought, there was no one there but me, I grabbed my head!

I was standin' there a-wond'rin' if I mighta lost my mind, when this girl crawled out from underneath my bed!

Hadn't happened in a while, so I looked her in the eye, and I asked her, "What're you doin' under there?"

She cried out, "Oh, you don't remember," and she broke down into tears, I was so surprised all I could do was stare!

Then she raised her little hand, and she waved it in my face, and I saw this pretty shiny diamond ring!

She said, "You flew us out to Vegas and you married me last night!" How do I get myself into this kinda thing?

Oh my goodness, won't somebody tell me what to do, I got married in the Elvis Room last night!

I'm sure I musta thought it was a good idea back then, but this mornin' something just ain't seemin' right!

I guess this is the reason Momma used to tell me, "Son, don't be hangin' out in bars and gettin' tight!"

But it's a little late to listen to what Momma told me now, I got married in the Elvis Room last night!

She stormed out to the kitchen and I followed her and tried to talk the sitchy-ation over sensibly,

But she just wouldn't listen, she was cryin' even more, she said, "Last night you said you fell in love with me!"

So I tried to break it gently, "I don't even know your name!", and the tears went flyin' all around the room,

And I knew I better think of somethin' quick before I drown, so I said, "Where we goin' on our honeymoon?"

Oh my goodness, won't somebody tell me what to do, I got married in the Elvis Room last night!

I'm sure I musta thought it was a good idea back then, but this mornin' something just ain't seemin' right!

I guess this is the reason Momma used to tell me, "Son, don't be hangin' out in bars and gettin' tight!"

But it's a little late to listen to what Momma told me now, I got married in the Elvis Room last night!

Well, now it's six months later, I've quit drinkin' and I think that there just might be somethin' good here after all,

The honeymoon was perfect and her name is Lori Sue, she's a soft and cuddly livin' lovin' doll!

You know I knew a lot of women in my wild and single days, but I never found the one I thought was right,

Till the night before I called my Momma on the phone and told 'er, "I got married in the Elvis Room last night!"

The band had gotten so into the song that, when Sam paused between the second and third verse, they'd automatically gone into a bridge that had them all dancing as they played, and Indie and Kenzie were even up on their feet. When Sam finished singing, they rolled it into a close that fit perfectly, and Sam couldn't help doing his Elvis impersonation: *"Thank ya, thank ya very much!"*

"Whoo hoo!" Chris yelled, and Stan said, "Man, that's awesome!" All four girls echoed them, and Sam jokingly took a bow.

Indie said, "Sam, what about the one you played for me, No Happy Endings? I'd love to hear what the band can do with that one!"

Chris said, "Let 'er rip, man," so Sam played through the first verse and chorus for them, and then they tried it together.

You all remember the story, you heard a long time ago,

The prince was throwin' a party, but Cinderella couldn't go,

Then a miracle happened, and she attended after all,

And by the time it was over, Cindy was the Queen of the Ball!

But there was more to the story, and if the truth was ever told,

You'd learn that hap'ly ever after, turned into somethin' cruel and cold,

And if you're wonderin' how I know, what I'm talkin' about,

I'm the prince who once was charming, till Cinderella threw me out!

There ain't no happy endings,
There ain't no ever afters,
Why don't we stop pretending,
With all the lies and laughter?
You know it's only in the moo—oo—vies,
Where the boy gets the girl,
There ain't no happy endings,

Out in the real world!

You know your mama always told you, that love was waitin' at your door,
And all you gotta do is find it, and you'll be happy evermore,
But you know it's just a fairy tale, like little children love to hear,
Let's leave the stories for the children, and cry our lonely, grown-up tears!

There ain't no happy endings,
There ain't no ever afters,
Why don't we stop pretending,
With all the lies and laughter?
You know it's only in the moo—oo—vies,
Where the boy gets the girl,
There ain't no happy endings,
Out in the real world!

There ain't no happy endings,
There ain't no ever afters,
Why don't we stop pretending,
With all the lies and laughter?
You know it's only in the moo—oo—vies,

Where the boy gets the girl,
There ain't no happy endings,
Out in the real world!

Once again, the band was blown away. "Man, these are great! Country music is full of heartache and sadness, and that one's gonna be a hit, I can tell! What else you got?"

Sam played them a few more songs, and they worked them up, as well. Indie cried when they went through the song Sam had written for their wedding, and they all enjoyed practicing it again. They worked until the sun began to go down, and agreed to meet again the following day to rehearse more. With some cover tunes to fill in, they had a good show for that weekend and they knew it.

Sam, Indie and Kenzie climbed into the truck and went home, and Sam watched Dora the Explorer with Kenzie while Indie made what she called "Instant Italian Chicken;" this consisted of putting chicken breasts into a casserole dish, covering them with pizza sauce and smothering the whole thing with shredded mozzarella cheese, then sticking it into a three hundred and fifty degree oven for forty-five minutes. When it was getting close, she put on some green beans and broccoli, and Sam began making comments about how good it all smelled.

They came to the table, and Kenzie made them bow

their heads to say grace.

"God, thank you for our food, and for Daddy's singin'!" she said, and Indie echoed with "Amen!"

"So," Indie said as they dug in, "what are the other two cases about?"

Sam grinned. "Well, one of them is in your ballpark; that woman wants to know where her husband is hiding his money. According to her, he's got several million stashed somewhere, and trying to keep the court from knowing about it. I figure you should be able to find it, and we get a ten percent finder's fee on any of it we locate. The court will make him pay up to her if we can find it, and we get paid then."

"Cool!" Indie said. "That's right down my alley! And the other one?"

Sam glanced at Kenzie, who was busy slipping tiny pieces of chicken to the cat under the table and paying them no attention. "That's the one that's mixed up in Carl's case. This man came in and said his wife started acting weird a few months ago, and then disappeared. Well, it turns out that the reason she was acting weird was because she was stalking Carl Morris. When her husband woke up to find her missing from bed, she said she just couldn't sleep and went to take a drive and relax, but she was actually going to Carl's house and trying to get him to come out and talk to her. I don't know why, yet, but that's odd that my two cases are linked that way."

Indie nodded. "Yeah, it is," she said. "Have you got a

lot of info on the wife? I might be able to find something on her, too, if she's turned up anywhere. Even a Jane Doe body, though I hope that's not the case, could be matched up if I have enough data."

"I made a lot of notes, and we can always call the husband for more if we need it. Tomorrow I'm going to talk to Carl about her, but the detective on his case says Carl was out of town and clean for when she disappeared."

Indie cocked her head. "What if she disappeared to go to wherever he was, and he got fed up? If he knew no one knew where she was, he might—you know."

Sam shrugged. "It's possible, but the cops feel sure he had nothing to do with it. I'm not gonna rule it out until I'm sure, though. And in another bit of irony, both the husband and Carl have the same lawyer, Carol Spencer. That may get interesting, too, down the line." Sam shoved another bite of chicken into his mouth. "And incidentally, this is delicious!"

"Of course it is," she said with a grin. "I didn't grow up with a hippie mom for nothing! She's a wealth of quick and easy delicious recipes, and I soaked up all of 'em!"

"I can see a bigger belt in my future, then," Sam said with a grin. They finished up their dinner, including Samson the cat, who had decided that Italian Chicken was high on his list of favorite dishes, too, and Kenzie went to play while Sam and Indie went to the office.

Indie had decided to set up her computer in the office when they'd gotten back, saying that it was more professional than having it on their dining table, so they'd bought another small desk and set her up a work station there, then brought the printer and Sam's computer out there, as well. His big desktop computer was set up at his desk, and he'd used it earlier, but this time he pulled his chair over by Indie's desk, and watched as she began going through the information he'd gotten from Albert Corning and Juliette Connors.

"Herman," Indie said, referring to the program she'd written to do her searches and hacking for her, "is a multitasker, like me. I'll feed him all of Mrs. Connors' info on her husband and his investments, and let him start on that, then I'll give him all we've got on Mrs. Corning, too. He can run both searches at the same time."

"Just as long as he works cheap," Sam said, and Indie chuckled.

"He's sorta like you," she said. "He just likes to keep me happy."

Sam nodded. "That's my boy! He and I are on the same page!"

The computer gave a ding, and Indie looked at the screen. "Well, well," she said, "he's got hit on Alex Connors already. Look at this," she said, pointing to a line of information that Sam couldn't understand if his life depended on it. "Here's an offshore corporation

that's registered through three proxies, each one belonging to the one above it, but guess who owns the top one? Connors Dental of Denver, Inc. That's our guy." She leaned close to the screen. "Now, let's see what else we can find on him." She typed for a moment, and then turned Herman loose again.

"I'm just curious," Sam said, "but how did you come up with Herman's name?"

Indie snickered. "My mom used to play this one song a lot, Henry The Eighth. It was from an old band in the sixties named Herman's Hermits, and I always thought Herman was a cute name. If Kenzie had been a boy, she might have ended up a Herman."

Sam's eyebrows went up. "Lucky for her she was a girl," he said, and Indie kicked him playfully.

Another ding, and she turned her attention to the computer again. "Uh-oh," she said. "Got a hit on a body that could be Mrs. Corning. It was found in the woods outside of Telluride about three months ago. Get the picture he gave you, I'm gonna see if I can get a photo of the body."

Sam grabbed the picture of Albert and Annie Corning from his desk, and Indie produced a photo of the Jane Doe from the news story about it. Both of them breathed a sigh of relief when there were no similarities other than age, size and hair color. Jane Doe had a squat, round face, while Annie's was thinner and longer. It wasn't her.

"Okay, well, each one we eliminate is one we don't have to worry about, right? Herman will keep searching..."

Another ding, and this time is was on Alex Connors, again. Another offshore corporation he owned through numerous proxies. "This guy's pretty sharp," Indie said. "A normal asset search would never find these, not even from the feds."

"Yeah, but he didn't reckon on his wife hiring the PI whose wife is the world's best hacker!"

Indie pushed him. "I'm not the best, babe, not by a long shot. I just like that what I'm doing now is helping people out." She leaned back for a kiss, and got it. "Mmm, especially you!"

Sam grinned. "Me, too. Let's let Herman do his thing, and go spend some time with our little girl, shall we?"

Indie tapped a few more keys, and nodded, so they rose and went to the living room. Kenzie was in the floor with some dolls, while Samson was lounging on the couch and watching. The little gray cat glanced at them as they entered, decided they weren't bringing him any treats, and went back to watching Kenzie play. Sam picked him up and moved him to the recliner, so that he and Indie could have their usual spot on the couch, and Samson seemed to find it acceptable.

"Kenzie," Sam said, "wanna watch a movie?"

"I'm busy," the little girl answered without looking

up. "You and Mommy can."

Indie smiled, and picked up the remote. They scanned through the channel guide and chose a movie they thought they'd like—both of them were into action movies—and settled back to watch.

4

Kenzie fell asleep in the floor before the movie ended, so Indie carried her up to bed, then she and Sam went back to the office to check on Herman.

"I told him to look for bank records on any offshore companies that come back to Alex Connors," she told Sam, grinning at the screen. "Look what he's found." She clicked a link, and suddenly the screen was filled with data. Sam looked closely, and realized that it was a list of bank accounts, and the total of assets in all of them came to almost thirty-two million dollars.

"Okay," he said, "now how do we present this information in a way that will satisfy the court?"

Indie smiled. "Easy," she said, tapped a few keys, and suddenly the printer was spitting out sheets of paper. More than fifteen pages came out before it was done, and Sam looked at them to see that each one listed the

offshore company, its ownership all the way back to Alex's dental corporation, and the relevant banks and account numbers with the amount of money in each one. The documents were clear and concise, and would allow the court—and the IRS—to nail Connors for hiding assets. With all of this, Sam figured, Connors wasn't only looking at contempt of court—he was probably going to get federal jail time for tax fraud.

"Wow," he said. "This'll do it. If the government doesn't hit her too hard, we're looking at about one-point-five million in finder's fees, babe. If they do, we should still see half a million or so."

"I done good?"

"Oh, baby," Sam said, "you done did real good! Maybe we should stick to asset recovery, and forget all the other stuff!"

Indie smiled. "Nah, you'd get bored. Can't have that, now, can we?"

"Good point," Sam said, and kissed her. "Anything on Mrs. Corning?"

Indie tapped, and a new screen of data appeared. "We've got three more Jane Does—I'm looking for pictures, now," she said, and a moment later there were three photos on the screen, but none of them were Annie Corning. "Then there's a woman who was picked up in Indiana, apparently suffering from some form of amnesia; let's take a look at—nope, not her. This gal is one of those who doesn't want to be found, I think."

Sam nodded. "I'm beginning to think so, too," he said. "The question is, why not?" He shook his head. "See what we can get on Mr. Corning, find out if there's anything he isn't telling me that might shed light on this."

"Okay, I'll set Herman to looking into him overnight, and we can go to bed. I don't know about you, baby, but I'm beat."

Sam grinned at her. "Me, too," he said. "Bed sounds good."

Indie grinned back. "Fine, but we have to get some sleep, too!"

Morning came like it always does, and Sam rolled over to find that Indie was already up. He could smell coffee, so he got up and took a quick shower, then dressed in his usual jeans and polo shirt and went out to the kitchen. Kenzie was already at the table, and Samson was under it, waiting for his own secret breakfast.

"Something in here smells wonderful," Sam said as he went to get a cup. Indie slapped his hand and pointed to the table, where a steaming cup was already waiting for him.

"It should," she said. "I got up early to make hash brown casserole, another one of mom's easy recipes. Hash browns, scrambled eggs and sausage all mixed together, and baked in the oven for half an hour, and then I made sausage gravy to go over it. If you don't love it, I'll ring your neck!"

Sam grinned. "I sincerely doubt I'm in any danger of

not loving it," he said. "From the smell alone, I'd say it's gonna be the best thing I've eaten in at least twenty-four hours!"

Indie walked over and kissed him as he sat down at the table, and then went to take the casserole out of the oven. A moment later she set it onto the table, and added a pitcher of gravy, while Sam dished it out to all of their plates. He poured gravy over his own, and Kenzie nodded when he asked if she wanted some, so he poured it over hers, too, then over Indie's.

"God," Kenzie said, "thank you for Mommy making this good breakfast for us to eat, Amen!"

"Amen!" they both echoed, and they all dug in. Sam took one bite, and then started exaggeratedly moaning with pleasure, while Kenzie laughed at him.

"Daddy likes it," she said, and Sam nodded enthusiastically.

"This is absolutely delicious," he said. "Babe, you are the best cook ever!"

They chatted while they ate, and Sam said that he was going to go and speak with Carl Morris again that morning. He wanted to ask about Annie Corning, to find out just what the story was there. They finished breakfast, then set Kenzie up with the TV while Sam and Indie went out to the office to check on Herman.

Herman had been busy. Not only had he dug up almost everything about Albert Corning's life, but he had four more Jane Does—none of them turned out to be

Annie, and Sam and Indie breathed a sigh of relief—and another news story about a woman who seemed not to know who she was. Indie called up the story, and they both froze. The photo of the woman in question showed none other than Annie Corning!

Sam immediately went to his desk and called the police department in Coos Bay, Oregon, where the woman had been found wandering around the bay almost three months earlier. According to the story, fishermen had found her walking around and looking dazed, and when they asked her if she was okay, she had just stared at them. She hadn't said a word when police were called, just looking at them as if she didn't understand a word they were saying, and so several interpreters were brought in to try other languages, but she'd finally looked at a policewoman and said, "I don't know what you want me to say." She'd gone silent again after that, but when she was asked who she was, she only shrugged and began to cry. They'd taken her to the local hospital, but since she wasn't sick or injured, she'd been transferred to a mental facility, where she remained.

"Dispatch," came the answer.

"Hello, my name is Sam Prichard, and I'm a private investigator in Colorado. I'm working a case on a missing woman, and I've just come across a news story about the woman you folks found wandering around three months ago. Can you tell me if she's ever been identified?"

"One moment," she said, and Sam heard some old

classical music begin to play. A moment later, a woman's voice came on the line.

"You're calling about Jane Doe?" she asked.

"Yes, Ma'am," Sam said. "I'm Sam Prichard, a private investigator from Denver, and I believe she may be a missing woman I'm looking for. Can you tell me if she's been identified?"

"Well, if she had, I wouldn't call her Jane Doe, now, would I? Can you tell me who she is?"

"Well, I believe her name is Annie Corning," he said. "The photo on the news story looks like her, and she disappeared about a week before yours turned up. She'd been acting strangely for about a month before that, and no one had any idea where she'd gone, or why. Her husband is actually under investigation for possible murder in this case, so he hired me to try to locate her."

The woman was quiet a moment, and Sam figured that she was writing down what he was saying. "Well, I can give you the number of her doctor at the hospital in North Bend," she said. "That's where she is right now. I won't say anything to them, so you can handle this however you want, but I appreciate you giving me this information, Mr. Shepard."

"Prichard," Sam said automatically, but she was still talking. She gave him the number and told him to ask for Dr. Martinez, and hung up without saying goodbye.

He dialed the number she'd given him, but the person who answered said Dr. Martinez wouldn't be in

for another hour. Sam looked at his computer to see the time, and realized that it wasn't even eight o'clock in Oregon, yet, so he thanked her and said he'd call back. He turned to Indie, who was staring at her screen.

"Well, if it's her, we've got two cases done already," he said, but she held up a hand and motioned for him to come closer. He rolled his chair over beside her again, and she pointed at the screen.

"You know how it seemed odd that Carl's case and the Corning case were related?" she asked.

"Yeah," Sam said. "What about it?"

"Well, when I tell Herman to dig up everything he can on someone, he does," she said. "Albert and Annie Corning both had some dental work done about four months ago, and you wanna guess where they went?"

Sam's eyebrows went up. "Alex Connors?"

"Yep, but that's not all. Since we were searching things on Alex Connors, Herman went a little deeper and pulled up Connors Dental's entire patient list. Wanna guess who else is on it?"

Sam stared at her. "Don't tell me—Carl Morris?"

"Bingo!" Indie said. "He was in for a cleaning the morning of the killings, last week."

Sam sat there for a moment. "That's odd. I had him tell me about his last few days before the killings, and he never mentioned that at all."

"It's more than odd, Sam," Indie said. "There's

something sort of creepy about this, y'know? I mean, come on, what are the odds of you getting three cases in one day and all of them being related, somehow?"

Sam looked at her for a minute, then said, "I wonder if the Cornings are connected to Jimmy Smith. We know that both Carl and Mrs. Connors are, and that was enough of a stretch in itself, but now we've got Alex connected to both Carl and Mrs. Corning, both of whom may have displayed bizarre behaviors afterward. What I'm wondering is if there is some sort of connection between their visits to the dentist and the strange things they did, or seem to have done, after."

Indie called up Connors Dental's website, and began looking through it. "Sam," she said, "Connors uses hypnosis instead of chemical anesthesia."

Sam looked where she was pointing, but shook his head. "Honey, it's been pretty well established that hypnosis can't make someone do something they wouldn't normally do. I don't think that's the connection we're looking for."

"No, but what about the drugs and alcohol in Carl's system? That drug they found, Adivol, is really zolpidem, and if we look it up, it's listed as a hypnotic. It's been known to cause people to do things they don't remember doing, and wouldn't do under normal circumstances. Look at this warning, right on their label: 'After taking Adivol, you may get up out of bed while not being fully awake and do an activity that you do not

know you are doing. The next morning, you may not remember that you did anything during the night... Reported activities include: driving a car ("sleep-driving"), making and eating food, talking on the phone, having sex, sleep-walking.' And there are cases of people even killing people and not knowing it."

Sam looked at her. "Babe, are you serious?"

"Here's a man named Robert Stewart who walked into a nursing home in North Carolina and shot eight people to death, and a woman who took the pill and then got up in the middle of the night and got in her car and ran over and killed a woman. Both of them got reduced sentences because they weren't in control of themselves, and there are others who have been acquitted of manslaughter and murder! The effect is even worse if alcohol is involved, it says. People have been known to do things like eating buttered cigarettes, and it's one of the most commonly used date rape drugs of all, now! When you're on it, you lose inhibitions against doing things you know you shouldn't, and since you don't remember what you've done, there's no guilt. Most of the date rape victims never know what happened to them, or they just think they decided to have sex on a whim."

Sam shook his head. "Okay, I can see how it could be barely possible that Carl might have really killed his family on this stuff," he said, "but where does Annie Corning fit in? She seems to have lost her memory..."

"Yeah, and check this out," Indie said quickly. "Eminem, the rapper, says that Adivol wiped out five years of his memory while he was on it. He says, 'a lot of my memory is gone. I don't know if you've ever taken Adivol, but it's kind of a memory-eraser.' He claims that he sees video of himself during that period, and has no memory of his performances or anything else. Yes, it can wipe out memory, and I'd bet that there's a way to make it do that, even if no one has ever said so."

Sam was staring at her, listening to all the information she was throwing at him. His mind was racing, and the more he heard, the more he wondered if the connection between the cases might be far more sinister than he'd ever dreamed possible. Could it be that someone, possibly Connors, was actually using zolpidem and alcohol to entice people to commit such heinous acts, or to literally erase their memories?

Sam looked at the time. "I'm going to call Mrs. Connors and let her know that we've got her report ready, then I'm gonna call that Dr. Martinez again in a little while. Once we know for sure whether the Jane Doe is Annie, we can figure out how to handle that, but right now I'm thinking that I want to talk to Carl first. I want to know what the connection between him and Annie was, and then I might even talk to Alex Connors, himself."

Indie looked at him. "Don't let him near your teeth, and if he asks you to look into his eyes, shoot him!"

Sam called Mrs. Connors' number, and she answered immediately. "Mr. Prichard?" she asked.

"Yes, Ma'am," he said. "I've got your report on your husband's offshore assets ready. If you'd like to come and pick it up, my wife Indie will be here most of the day, or I can fax it to you, if you prefer."

"Wow, already? Can you tell me what you found?"

"Yes, he's got a number of offshore companies with a total of about thirty-two million in various bank accounts. I think that fits with what you expected to find?"

She let out a shout of excitement. "Boy, does it ever! Thank you, thank you so very much! Yes, if you would, you can just fax it to my attorney, Carol Spencer. Just a moment, let me get the number!" She was off the line for a moment, then came back and gave him a fax number. "I can't thank you enough," she said, "or I guess I can, when we get this into court! Alex will be paying both of us, then! Woo-*hoo!*"

Sam laughed and hung up, then put the stack of reports into his fax machine and dialed the number. Moments later the sheets began feeding in and through it, and that job was done.

Sam looked at the time again and saw that it had been almost an hour since he'd called Oregon, so he dialed the number again. This time he was put through, and a slightly accented woman's voice said, "This is Dr. Martinez."

"Dr. Martinez, my name is Sam Prichard, and I'm a

private investigator from Colorado. I'm looking for a woman who went missing a few months ago, and I have reason to believe she may be your Jane Doe."

"Oh, really?" the doctor said. "Can you tell me who she is? She's been quite a mystery to us, here."

"I believe her name is Annie Corning, and she disappeared three months ago, after some strange behavior that lasted about a month prior to her disappearance. Can you tell me how she's doing?"

The doctor sighed. "I wish I could tell you," she said, "but all she does is sit and stare out the windows. Our staff says it's all they can do sometimes to get her to eat, and she rarely even speaks. Is she married?"

"Annie is, yes. Her husband's name is Albert. No kids."

"Let me go and talk to her, and see if any of this might jog a memory. Give me a number and I'll call you back. Do you know of any identifying marks?"

"No, none were mentioned, but I'll find out and let you know." He gave her his number and said goodbye, with a promise to ask Albert about any scars or birthmarks.

He turned back to Indie. "It might well be her. The doctor is going to talk to her, see if she remembers Albert or her own name." He sighed. "If she's had her mind wiped out somehow..."

"Yeah," Indie said. "What will it take to help her get it back?"

Sam nodded. "I'm going to see Carl. I'll call you when I get done there." He kissed her, and then went out through the house so he could give Kenzie a hug goodbye, as well. Once that was done, he got onto his motorcycle and rode off toward the detention center.

When he walked in, the jailer looked up and smiled. "Here to see Mr. Morris? Just a moment, I'll get someone up here right away." Sam stood and waited only a minute before the same female jailer came to escort him to the interview room. He was there less than thirty seconds when Morris was brought in and chained to the table.

"Sam," Morris said. "Is this good news?"

"I'm not sure, yet, Carl. I wanted to ask you a couple of things. First, the other day you told me about the last few days before what happened, remember?"

Carl nodded. "Yes, sure," he said. "Why?"

Sam watched him closely. "Well, I'm curious why you didn't tell me about going to the dentist to get your teeth cleaned that morning. Do you remember that?"

Carl Morris cocked his head to one side. "Dentist? I —yes, I remember. Huh. I wonder why that slipped my mind before?" He looked confused. "Does it matter?"

Sam shrugged. "I'm not sure," he said. "Can you tell me about it now?"

Carl smiled. "Sure. I go to Dr. Connors, he's about the best around here, and he isn't into chemicals and drugs. He uses hypnosis, instead, and for me that's

important because I don't like using any kind of medicines. He put me under, cleaned my teeth, and then woke me up and I was done. No big deal, I've been through it a few times before."

Sam watched him, but couldn't see any sign that Carl was being evasive or untruthful, so he moved on. "Okay, now, what can you tell me about Annie Corning? I understand you had some problems with her a while back?"

Carl's face went sour. "Oh, Lord," he said, "did I ever! It was a few months ago, she and I met at the Mary Williams home—I go there and work with some of the boys, teaching them about bodybuilding and weightlifting. She was helping out there, and we got to be friends, but then one day she started telling me all this weird stuff, real wild things like how aliens were trying to get into her mind, and wanting to make her do things. I said she might want to see someone, you know, like a shrink, but she kept saying she needed to talk to me, because they were after me next." He rubbed his free hand over his chin. "She was pretty wild. It got to where she was following me around, and then she started showing up at my house at night, sometimes really late at night. My wife was so mad she couldn't..." His voice trailed off for a moment, and then he shook his head. "She got so mad that she asked me to stop working with the kids, but I said I couldn't do that. Instead, I talked to Mrs. Peters at the home, and she got Annie assigned to different days than me, and that took care of part of it,

but she still came to my house a few times. I finally told her that if she didn't stop, I'd go to the police. She came once more after that and I pretended to call the cops, and she left. I never saw her again, and I heard she ran out on her husband, but then there were rumors he'd killed her. I don't know him, so I just stayed out of it."

"Okay, I heard you went to some competition in California, and were there when she disappeared, is that right?"

Carl shrugged. "I'm not sure if that's when she left, but I never saw her again after that."

Sam sat there and looked at him for a moment. "Carl, have you ever had any other strange episodes, where you did something but don't remember it? Maybe in the middle of the night?"

Carl stared at him. "Well, not that I—well, there was one time, almost a year ago. I went to bed that night, and when I woke up, I was in my neighbor's pool, swimming around as naked as a newborn. It was about three in the morning, and I was lucky no one saw me." He looked down at the table, and then back up to Sam. "Sam, is there something wrong with me? Am I like, a split personality or something? I mean, that's the only time I can remember anything like that, but what if there were other times, and I just don't know about them? Maybe I've been doing strange things my whole life, and when I..."

Sam reached out and touched his hand on the table.

"Whoa, hold on. I need you to focus for a minute, here. Is there any chance you can recall what all you did the day before that happened, the swimming incident?"

Carl shook his head. "No, I don't think so, but I can tell you the exact date," he said. "I know the date because it was the night before my wife's birthday, and I was scared to death that someone had seen me and would call her and tell her! It was August twenty-second, last year."

Sam wrote the date down on his note pad. "Okay, Carl," he said, "I think that covers it at the moment—oh, wait. Just out of curiosity, you know Jimmy Smith, the talent agent?"

Carl smiled sadly. "Yes," he said. "We go way back, he's my agent. He's gotten me a few small movie roles, and helped me get into some of the bigger competitions. He's the one who told me to call you; he said when he was accused of murder, you were the only one who was willing to dig down and find the truth, so if there was anyone who could figure out why I did this, it'd be you."

Sam thanked him and signaled for the jailer to come and let him out. Like always, they took Carl out first, and then the lady jailer walked Sam out.

"Do you think he did it?" she asked when they were alone in the hallway.

Sam shrugged. "At this point, all I can say is it's possible he did, but was under the influence of a drug, and it may have been given to him without his

knowledge. I'm still digging, but I'm convinced that it was not a premeditated murder. That doesn't mean he isn't guilty, just that it might not be something he would have done, had he been in his own right mind."

She nodded. "That's kind of what I'm thinking," she said, "like maybe he was—I dunno, possessed, or something."

Sam stared at her as if struck by how much sense her comment had made. "That may be the best analogy I've heard for it, yet," he said as he left her.

He got outside and called Indie. "Babe," he said when she answered, "I want you to check something for me. See if Carl went to see Dr. Connors anytime close to August twenty-second of last year, and let me know."

"Okay, hang on," she said. "I'm at the computer now, so gimme a sec—August twenty-second, Connors' calendar is coming up—August twenty-second, yes! He was there to get a cap replaced. Why?"

"Because, late that night, he went for a moonlight skinny-dip in his neighbor's pool, and woke up while he was swimming around in it. He got away without being seen, but it's the only other time he could recall ever doing anything strange. He'd gone to bed, and then woke up swimming around in his birthday suit, so it shook him up."

"And he went to see Connors that day, too. Sam, this is getting more and more weird."

"I'm pretty sure there's a connection," Sam said, "but

we still have to find out what it is and prove it. I'm going to go and see Connors, and ask a few questions."

"Okay, but be careful. If this guy's some kind of Svengali, don't you come home trying to kill me, or I'll beat your brains in with a skillet!"

"Trust me, babe," Sam said, "I have no intention of letting him give me any kind of treatments!"

5

Sam hung up from talking to Indie, and his phone rang instantly. He looked at the number and recognized it as being from the hospital in Oregon.

"Sam Prichard," he said.

"Mr. Prichard, this is Dr. Martinez in North Bend," came the doctor's voice. "I wanted to tell you that our Jane Doe is your Annie Corning. I went to her a bit ago and said, 'Annie, are you ready to eat?' and she turned around and looked at me and said, 'Yes, I'm starving!' She says she knows that's her name, but she doesn't remember her husband yet, and nothing else is coming back, but she's been quite animated and talkative since then."

"Well, that's a start, anyway. I'll contact her husband right now and let him know. Can he come up to see her?"

"Oh, I think that would be a wonderful idea, but you might have him call me, first. I'm not sure she'll be ready or able to leave, just yet. First, I'm sure she's going to want to try to remember her life with him." She paused for a moment. "Mr. Prichard, is there any reason to believe that there were problems between them? Any kind of abuse, perhaps?"

"None that I know of, and I don't think there was anything like that. On the other hand—Doctor, maybe you can help me. I'm working on a couple of cases now, and hers may be one of them, that seem to indicate that someone is deliberately tampering with people's minds, using zolpidem, possibly combined with alcohol and hypnosis. Have you ever heard of anything like that?"

"Oh, dear heavens, Mr. Prichard," she said. "No, I haven't, but as a clinical hypnotist myself, I can tell you that the very thought of it suddenly terrifies me! Zolpidem is a powerful drug, with serious effects on our inhibitions. If a small dose were given to someone who was already in trance, and suggestions planted to take more at a later time—my God, it's conceivable that a post-hypnotic suggestion could be planted that would override all of our natural inhibitions!"

Sam sighed. "I was afraid you'd say that. Doctor, it's very possible that Annie Corning was treated in this way. Could such a suggestion possibly result in wiping her memory?"

"I couldn't say with any reasonable certainty, but I

75

would hazard a guess that it is possible, yes. What concerns me even more, however, is how to formulate any kind of recovery program for her; I'd have no concept of where to begin!"

"I'm going now to try to speak to the person I believe is behind this," Sam said. "I don't know if I'll get any answers that will help you or not, but I'll let you know if I get any at all. Right now, I'm going to call Annie's husband and give him your number. And Doctor, I'm not going to tell him what I suspect just yet; I'm gonna imply that the problem might be a side effect of medication. Can you cover me on that for a bit, till I know for sure what I'm dealing with?"

"Certainly, Mr. Prichard," the doctor said. "I won't say anything until I hear from you."

He ended the call and looked in his notes for Albert Corning's number, then dialed it. Corning answered almost immediately.

"Hello?"

"Al, this is Sam Prichard," Sam said. "I'm calling to tell you that I've found your wife."

Corning gasped. "Oh, God, Sam, is she—is she alive?"

Sam sighed into the phone. "She's alive, Al, but there are complications. Annie is in a hospital in Oregon, and has amnesia. Until just a bit ago, she didn't even know her own name, and at the moment, she doesn't remember being married or who you are. I have the

number of her doctor for you, and she'd like you to call as soon as possible."

Corning said, "Oh, my God, oh, my God—I'll call right now! Let me get a pen, oh, my God! This is—Sam, how can I thank you? Can I tell the police? Can I tell her sister?"

"I think you should take that up with her doctor, but I'm sure she'll be glad to confirm for them that your wife is alive and in her care. Now, there's something else I want to talk to you about; you and Annie went to get some dental work a short time before she began acting strangely, do you remember that?"

"Dental work? Yeah, sure, I got a check-up and Annie got a crown and a couple of fillings. Why?"

"And Annie started acting strangely right after that?"

Corning was quiet for a moment, as if thinking, then said slowly, "Well, yes. Is there a connection?"

"Well, I happen to be looking at another case, where it's possible that there is a side effect of the dentist's hypnotic anesthesia, combined with other things, that might cause some kinds of amnesia. I just want you to be aware that this isn't Annie's fault, none of it."

Corning sighed. "Sam—thank you. I don't know what else to say, so I'll just say thank you! I'll call the doctor now, what's the number?"

Sam gave him the number and hung up, then Googled the dentist's office address. He got onto the Shadow and rode that way.

* * * * *

Indie was worried, but if there was one thing she knew about Sam, it was that he could take care of himself. She went about her daily routine, cleaning up the house, thinking about what to make for dinner and keeping one mother's eye on Kenzie, with another watching that cat! Samson was a pretty good kitty, but every now and then, he'd get it in his head that he was a climber. She'd found him on top of the refrigerator, on top of the cabinets, and once he got on top of the long curtain rod that was over the sliding glass doors leading to the back yard.

Climbing up, it seemed, he was good at. Getting back down always involved Indie having to stand on a chair and coax him into reach.

Still, having the cat had been good for Kenzie. After some of the hard times they'd been through, during which the child never once complained, Indie was thankful for their new lives, for the stability that Sam had brought to them, for the love and happiness that the three of them shared. She often caught herself whispering, "Thank you, Lord," as she went about her day, and the sense of peace that would come over her made her feel that He was answering, "You're welcome."

She'd just finished running the vacuum in the living room when her phone rang again, and she glanced to see that it was her mother. She rolled her eyes; she loved her mom, but they talked at least three or four times a day,

usually. She answered the call with a smile she didn't necessarily feel.

"Hey, Mom," she said.

"Indie," her mother began, "I know how Sam feels about Beauregard, but he insists I call and tell you this anyway."

A chill went down Indie's spine. Beauregard was the ghost of a Confederate soldier who was supposedly her mother's "spirit guide." He was also, she firmly believed, a figment of her mother's imagination, but somehow, he seemed to know things, and as long as Indie had been alive, he hadn't been wrong once when he predicted something. She was sure the truth was that her mother had some gift for prognostication, but used Beauregard as the way she dealt with it.

"What is it, Mom?" she asked, dreading the answer. Beauregard had a tendency to predict bad news.

"Well, Beauregard says that Sam is about to be in a lot of trouble, and that it's going to be up to you to save him. That's all he'll tell me, he says, the rest of it you have to find out yourself."

Indie's breath caught, but she forced it. "Okay, Mom, I'm gonna call Sam now and warn him. He'll get mad, but I'll do it anyway! Bye!" She hung up and dialed Sam's phone.

It rang four times and went to voicemail, which probably meant he was on the motorcycle and rolling down the road, so he didn't hear the phone. She hung

up and tried again, but this time when it went to voicemail, she said, "Sam, call me! Urgent!" and hung up, praying he'd see the missed call and get back to her quickly.

* * * * *

Sam rode up to the dental building, parked the Shadow and got off. His leg was bothering him a bit, so he pulled the cane out of the holster he'd made for it on the front forks and went inside. A chubby, blonde receptionist greeted him cheerfully, and Sam made a joking bet with himself that she was hired by Mrs. Connors, and would probably be replaced as soon as the divorce was final.

"Hi, and welcome to Connors Dental. How can we help you today?"

Sam smiled. "I'd like to speak with Dr. Connors for a moment," he said, holding out his ID. "My name is Sam Prichard, I'm a private investigator."

The girl's eyes grew large, and she picked up a phone. "Dr. Connors?" she said after a moment. "There's a private investigator her who would like to speak with you." She listened for about five seconds, then said, "Yes, sir." She hung up the phone and said, "He'll be right out."

A door in the wall behind her opened only seconds later, and a portly, balding man of medium height in a white dentist's smock stepped out. "I'm Dr. Connors," he said. "How can I help you?"

Sam kept his face stoic, but shook the offered hand. "Doctor, I'm Sam Prichard, and I'm a private investigator. I'd like to talk to you about a couple of your patients who seem to be having some problems after seeing you."

Connors' eyebrows went up. "Problems? Come on back to my office, please." He glanced at the receptionist, who seemed to be ignoring them completely, and led Sam through the door and down a hallway. The office was only a short distance away, and he pointed to a comfortable chair when they got inside with the door closed behind them.

"Now," he said, "can you tell me what this is about?"

"Dr. Connors, two of your patients have exhibited some bizarre behavior shortly after being here for your services. One of them is Annie Corning, who began acting strangely right after getting some work done four months ago, and then disappeared completely a month later. She's just been found, alive, but with seemingly complete amnesia. The other is Carl Morris, who is sitting in jail right now for the brutal murders of his wife and children. He saw you for a cleaning under hypnosis the morning of the day it happened."

Connors didn't show any emotion during Sam's recital of the facts. "I'm sorry, I don't see how either of these situations has anything to do with me."

Sam narrowed his eyes. "You don't? Doesn't it seem odd to you that both of these people started acting oddly

right after seeing you? That would be a coincidence that would worry me, if I were in your shoes. Suppose their behavior is a side effect of your hypnosis? That could be devastating to your business, if the word got out, and if Carl Morris is able to bring it up as a defense in his murder trial, it's going to be all over the front pages of an awful lot of newspapers, I can guarantee you. Now, don't you want to try to enlighten me about how your hypnosis works, so I can go back and say that I didn't find any connection? Or would you rather I go to the prosecutor with what I've got so far, and let him draw his own conclusions?"

Connors smiled. "Mr. Prichard, I didn't mean to give the impression I don't care, and of course I want to help, but there is a long established fact, and that is that no one will do anything under hypnosis they wouldn't do by their own choice. If Mr. Morris was here that morning, and I've seen the accounts of his crime in the newspapers and TV, then he would have been completely free of any hypnotic suggestion long before the murder took place. And as for the lady you mentioned, no amount of hypnosis can erase a memory for more than a short time. It's been tried, in clinical cases where people wanted to forget past traumas; it can't be done."

Sam nodded. "Not on its own, no," he said, "but I'm working on the theory that there might be psychoactive and hypnotic medications involved. Mr. Morris had a large dosage of zolpidem in his system. Zolpidem is

better known as Adivol, Dr. Connors, in case you're not aware of that, and it's been associated with many different kinds of bizarre behaviors including a number of murders and accidental killings. I've spoken with a psychiatrist who says it's quite likely that if a dose were given to a person while under hypnosis, the combined effect could cause a suggestion to override the natural inhibitions against doing whatever was suggested."

Connors didn't even blink. "I can see where that might be possible," he said, "but that's why it has nothing to do with me. We don't use any kind of chemical anesthesia here other than locals—benzocaine, novocaine, the normal stuff any dentist uses. I don't even use nitrous oxide here, because I don't believe it offers any real benefit."

"In that case, you wouldn't object to me taking a look around? Just to confirm that you don't have any kinds of drugs here?"

Connors smiled. "Mr. Prichard, I may be cooperative, but I'm not a fool. If a search is to be made, I'm afraid it will have to be done by the police, and with a lawful search warrant. If you can get the police to believe this crazy story, they're more than welcome to come here, warrant in hand, and look to their hearts' content. Until then, I believe we're done talking." He stood up. "I'll show you out."

Sam rose to his feet and looked Connors in the eye. "I'll go, no problem, but I will be back with the police

and that warrant. And I'll also tell you this: if I find proof that you are manipulating the minds of people with hypnosis and drugs, I will see to it that you are buried so deep in the prison system that you'll forget what daylight even looked like." He turned to go through the door, and heard the doctor step forward to follow.

* * * * *

Sam sat up, wiping his face and feeling something wet on it. He looked around, wondering where he was, and suddenly froze. He was sitting on the floor, and beside him was a woman with her back to him. She was covered in blood, and he instinctively reached out to turn her over, so he could see who she was.

It was Juliette Connors, and she was quite dead, he could tell. She'd been shot through the head, and the bullet was apparently a fairly large caliber one; most of the top of her head was gone, along with most of the brain tissue that used to be in it. Sam stared at her, wondering how he'd come to be there, and who had killed his client.

He reached for his phone to call 911, but even as he started to dial, he heard sirens and vehicles roaring up outside of wherever he was. He climbed to his feet and looked around, realizing he was in a house. He saw the front door, and took two steps toward it before it came crashing in.

A policeman stood there, his gun in his hand, and he was shouting at Sam to get down on his knees and put

his hands behind his head. Sam complied automatically, his mind racing, and then he was being wrestled to the floor. His hands were wrenched cruelly behind his back, and handcuffs were applied, even as he was trying to tell the officers who were surrounding him that he had just woke up there, that he was trying to call them when they showed up, but they weren't listening.

One of them rolled him over onto his back, and looked down at him.

"Samuel Prichard," he said, "you are under arrest for the murder of Juliette Connors. You have the right to remain silent. If you give up the right to remain silent, anything you say can and will be used against you in a court of law. You have the right to have an attorney present during questioning. If you cannot afford an attorney..."

Sam knew the drill, and shut his mouth. He had no clue what was going on, but he was sure he hadn't killed anyone, and he wasn't going to risk saying something they could use to make him look guilty. He'd go to jail, just as he'd taken numerous others to jail, and then figure out what was going on.

And then he'd call Indie.

He was hauled out and stuffed into the back seat of a cruiser, and left alone there for a while, the engine running and the AC on. He sat there and tried to remember what had happened. He'd gone to see Dr. Connors, and confronted him about the drug-hypnosis

connection, which had been denied. He was just leaving when—that's when he woke up.

Dear God, he thought, *the bastard's done it to me! But how? I didn't go under hypnosis, and I didn't take or drink anything while I was there...*

The only possible answer was that he was drugged suddenly, possibly with something that put him down without a fight. He knew it wouldn't be chloroform—despite its popularity with crime fiction authors and movie producers, actual unconsciousness from chloroform takes about five minutes of inhalation, during which time the victim is usually objecting violently. Sam knew that there were other drugs, though, that could render someone senseless in a matter of seconds, and suspected that one had been used on him.

He couldn't see a clock, so he had no idea how much time had passed since he left the dentist's office. If it had been more than just a few minutes, it was probably enough time that there would be no trace of any drugs or chemicals to be found there, because the man's first logical move would be to get rid of everything that could implicate him. If Sam began talking about his theories, he'd sound like a lunatic, and he knew it. Even the evidence he and Indie had compiled wouldn't be enough to convince a prosecutor.

Prosecutor—Sam had just been arrested for murder, and the worst part was that he couldn't be certain that he hadn't done it. If Connors was the cunning monster that

he and Indie suspected him to be, then it was quite possible that he had programmed Sam to go to his wife's home and kill her. With that thought in mind, Sam was fairly certain that the large caliber bullet that had killed Mrs. Connors would turn out to be a forty-caliber slug from his own weapon.

The police had been forced to break down the door, he remembered. That would indicate that, just like Carl Morris, the doors had been locked from the inside. If that were the case, then it was likely that Sam was the only possible suspect in this crime, and given the circumstances and without knowledge of the possible hypnotic connection, he'd believe it himself.

However, even if he had pulled the trigger and fired the fatal shot, Sam was not the killer—he was the murder weapon, just as Carl Morris had been the weapon that killed his own family. Since neither of them had any knowledge of what they had done, or in fact, whether they had done anything at all, and since neither of them had been complicit in taking whatever drugs were involved, a reasonable defense would likely be that they were not lawfully responsible, any more than a gun was responsible for the death of the person standing in front of it when its trigger was pulled.

There were numerous police officers present, and Sam saw Karen Parks, the homicide detective that he'd worked with on the Jimmy Smith case. She looked at him as she walked past the car, but there was none of the friendliness he recalled from that time. He watched her

go into the house, and when she came out twenty minutes later, she was carrying a zip-lock bag with a gun in it. He knew he'd been right as soon as he saw it; the black and white grips were the ones Danny Jacobs had given him once for a birthday present. The murder weapon they were focused on was his own gun.

She walked up to the car and opened the door beside him. "Sam," she said, "I'm sure you know I hate this, but I've gotta say, this is one ugly mess you've handed me. Want to tell me what happened?"

Sam looked at her, wishing he could tell her all of it, but he knew she'd think he was either nuts, or lying to try to save his own skin. Since he'd been hired by Mrs. Connors to find her husband's assets, a case could be made that he might have made a deal with Connors to kill her so that he wouldn't have to share his wealth. Granted, that would implicate Connors, but it would make an even stronger case against Sam, so it wasn't a line of thought he wanted anyone else to consider. He looked up at Karen and said, "I hate this too, but I think I need a lawyer before I say anything."

She nodded and closed the door, turning her back and walking away. Sam felt terribly alone, just then, and wished with all his heart that Dan Jacobs were still alive. At least then, he figured, there would be one person on the force who wouldn't believe he was a cold-blooded killer.

A few minutes later, a policeman got into the front

seat and said, "I hear you're an ex-cop. That true?"

Sam said, "Yes."

The officer shook his head. "They're gonna have fun with you in prison," he said, then started the car and drove out toward the detention center. The last thing Sam noticed as they drove away was that his motorcycle wasn't in the driveway.

The cop pulled the car into the Sally Port at the detention center, and got out to lock his weapon into a locker on the wall before he opened the door and reached in to help Sam stand up. Sam's hip gave a sharp twinge, and he almost fell, but the officer held him up.

"No games," he said. "We're going inside to booking, don't give me any trouble."

"I'm not," Sam growled. "I took three bullets to my hip, and it still gives me trouble. I'm okay now."

They waited for the jailer on duty to buzz them in, and Sam was escorted past the detention center's operations desk and to a holding cell. The cuffs were removed, and Sam went directly to the pay phone on the wall. He fumbled in his pocket for change, and shoved fifty cents into the phone, then dialed Indie's number.

"Hello?" she said, not recognizing the number.

"Baby, it's me," Sam said, and Indie began talking fast.

"Oh, God, Sam, where are you? Why aren't you on your own phone? I know you're gonna get mad, but Mom called, and said Beauregard said to tell you you're

about to be in trouble..."

Sam sighed. "Well, you can tell her he was right again. Indie, I can't tell you all of it on the phone, but I've been arrested for the murder of Juliette Connors. All I know right now is that I woke up lying on the floor beside her body, but it looks like I did it, after leaving the last person I told you I was going to see. As far as I know, she was shot to death with my gun, but I don't remember anything after talking to you-know-who."

Indie let out a sob. "Oh, my God, Sam," she said, her voice desperate. "Sam, what do I do?"

"The first thing I need you to do is get me an attorney, fast. In this case, I think I need the same one Carl's using, Carol Spencer. That's also the lawyer Mrs. Connors was using for her divorce, so she may object, but ask her to come and see me as soon as possible. Give her a retainer, whatever she wants; I need her fast."

Indie was crying. "Okay, Sam, I'll call her right now. Can you call me back in a few minutes?"

"I don't know if I can or not, babe, but I'll call you as soon as I'm able. I love you."

"Oh, Sam, I love you too! I know you didn't do this, babe, and we'll prove it, I swear!" She sighed into the phone, and Sam's heart was breaking at the pain he could hear in her voice. "Beauregard said I was gonna have to be the one to save you."

"Well, for once, it's okay to do what Beauregard says. In fact, if he's got any advice, I'm willing to listen!"

"I'll call the lawyer now, and then I'll call Mom and ask. I love you, Sam. I'll talk to you soon!"

She hung up, and Sam did likewise, then went to the little bathroom area and looked into the steel mirror. There was blood on his face, neck and hands, so he rinsed it off the best he could, then took a seat on a bench. He was feeling a little tired, but other than that, he couldn't detect any notable side effects of whatever drugs had been used on him. He hoped the lawyer would get there soon, because he wanted his blood tested immediately. He didn't know how long it took for zolpidem to get out of his system, so he didn't even want to go to the bathroom before that.

6

Sam sat there for about half an hour and was thinking about calling Indie back when his name was called. He looked up to see the female jailer who'd been escorting him to see Carl standing at the door of the cell, just staring at him.

"Yes?" he asked.

"Mr. Prichard," she said slowly, "you've got an attorney here to see you. I need you to turn around so I can cuff you, sir."

Sam did as she directed, knowing that it was simply procedure, and she took him by the arm and led him to that same interview room. An older woman with glasses was sitting inside waiting, and when he'd been cuffed to the table, she introduced herself.

"Mr. Prichard," she said, "I'm Carol Spencer. I've been expecting to talk to you, but this isn't what I'd

envisioned. Carl Morris said you were supposed to get with me about your retainer yesterday."

"Yeah," Sam said, "I've been kind of busy. Thanks for coming so quickly. Did my wife happen to give you any background on the cases I've been working on?"

Carol smiled. "That girl can talk faster than any client I've ever had," she said. "She told me a lot, including your theories about what happened to Mr. Morris, and to Annie Corning, and that you and she think something similar happened to make you kill one of my other clients." She sat and looked at him for a moment, and he was about to speak, when she went on. "The funny thing is, I believe it. Every word. I've known Alex Connors for years, and this wouldn't be the first time I've been on the opposite side of a courtroom from him. I represented a couple of women who claim that he sexually assaulted them some time back. They claimed something similar, that they would suddenly wake up in bed with him, and he'd tell them that they ran into each other somewhere, and the ladies couldn't keep their hands off him. Unfortunately for my clients, there were witnesses and security footage that made it clear that he was telling the truth. I often wondered if his hypnosis was involved, but psychiatric experts all say that isn't possible."

"It isn't," Sam said, "under normal hypnosis, but when drugs and alcohol are added into the mix, things get murkier. I want you to get my blood tested immediately. We're looking for zolpidem and alcohol."

"I've already got a nurse coming to draw your blood, should be any second now. I want to know what they find, too. You're aware that both of them were found in Carl's blood, right?"

Sam nodded. "Yeah, I know. That's what set me on this path. Then, when I found out that he'd been to Connors' office that morning, I began to think that there was a connection. When I found out that Annie Corning was there as well, just before she started acting weird, I was sure of it."

Carol nodded, and made a note on a pad she'd laid in front of her. "Tell me about your meeting with Connors."

"I went there unannounced, and he invited me back into his office. I told him my suspicions, which he denied, of course, and then I challenged him, asked if he'd be willing to let me look around. He said no, and told me to get police and a warrant if I thought I had a case, and that he was done talking to me. I started to leave, I remember, and the next thing I know, I'm in Mrs. C.'s house with her body laying beside me and blood on my hands. I saw that she was dead and took out my phone to call for help, and that's when I heard sirens right outside, so I got up and was going to the door when the cops bashed the door in. That's it."

Carol nodded and scribbled, and then they heard the door opening. A jailer stood there with a nurse.

"I'm supposed to draw blood," the nurse said, and

Carol nodded. She came in and Sam held out his free arm. Carol put a finger to her lips to tell him to be quiet until the nurse and jailer were gone.

The nurse drew three vials of blood from Sam, and he suppressed the urge to make vampire jokes; he wasn't in a laughing mood, of course. When she was done, she and the jailer left the room and he and Carol were alone again.

"Sam," she began, "can I call you Sam? Sam, I'm not gonna beat around the bush. Without some serious evidence, the best we can hope for with this defense is a reasonable doubt as to premeditation. Unless we can prove how any drugs, assuming we find any, got into your system, we can't be convincing as to a motive or a method or a perpetrator. The other problem we're going to run into is that I now have two clients who need this defense, yourself and Carl. If I try it twice in a row, with nothing to back it up other than the circumstantial evidence that both of you were at his office before the murders occurred, I'm going to get both of you sent to death row." She took off her glasses and rubbed her eyes. "Sam, is there anything else you can think of that might help us prove that Connors is behind this?"

Sam sat and thought, but couldn't come up with anything that he felt would make a difference. "The real problem is that I have no idea of his motives," he said. "I had already wondered if he was using Annie Corning for sex, and hearing about your previous clients makes me think I was on the right track, there, but why on earth

would he want Carl to kill his family? What possible motive could he have for doing this sort of thing to Carl?"

"Well, remember, zolpidem has its own nasty side effects. It's possible that Connors is using it for a less sinister purpose, like to make people more amenable to things he wants them to do, but that what happened with Carl was only a coincidence."

Sam nodded. "Yeah, I've considered that, but then we've got me. There's no doubt in my mind that I was programmed to go there, whether I actually killed her or not, and I think we have to assume I did. I can't imagine that he tried to get me to do something innocuous, but instead I went and shot his wife—which, incidentally, is awfully convenient since he was about to have to pay her a whopping lot of money! Did he know that, yet, I wonder?"

"Well, his lawyer did. I sent him copies of the documents you sent to me as soon as I got them. He'd have probably told Connors, and it's even possible that Connors knew who you were when he heard your name, since it was right there on the pages you faxed to me."

Sam rolled his eyes. "I hadn't thought of that, but then, he surely wouldn't have been expecting me. Somehow, he managed to knock me out fast and then program me, and I literally remember nothing. This guy is incredibly dangerous."

"Well, I'm not going to dispute that, but we still have

to prove it. Any bright ideas, there, Mr. Investigator?"

Sam sat there and hung his head for a minute, trying to think of anything that might help. Suddenly he looked up. "Maybe," he said. "What if we could get corroborating statements from other people who have experienced weird behavior after seeing him?"

Carol thought about it. "Well, if any of them happened to have gotten into some kind of trouble, actually broken the law by doing something that was convincingly out of character, that would be pretty powerful. I doubt we'll ever get to bring him to justice, though, because he's almost certain to disappear as soon as he finds out we're working on this as a defense, and especially if he knows there are others out there who could add fuel to our fires. If we can get a jury to believe that he's really doing these things, then it is very possible I can get you acquitted, in spite of the physical evidence." She thought for a moment. "Ironically, one of the women I represented is no longer living; she killed herself over the whole thing, poor kid. The other one I might be able to track down, and she could help, if she will. If it means another shot at hanging Connors, or at least proving she wasn't the slut he said she was, I think she'd do it."

Sam smiled. "Then you get the blood results and work on that, and I'll get my wife tracking down the rest of his patients from the past few years. Surely we'll find at least a few of them who have gotten into some kind of trouble, doing something they can't explain."

Carol nodded. "Okay, we've got one more thing to do while I'm here. Detective Parks from homicide wants to speak to you."

Sam nodded. "That's fine. I just said I wouldn't talk without a lawyer. Should I say anything about our suspicions?"

"I wouldn't go into detail about everything just yet, but you can certainly say that the last you remember, you were at her husband's office, and that you believe you've been framed. Let's keep it simple, we're dealing with a homicide detective; they don't always have the most open of minds."

Sam grinned and nodded, and Carol got up and tapped on the door. When the jailer opened it, she said, "We're ready for the detective," and he closed it again. Carol sat down again, but this time she took a chair next to Sam. Karen Parks came in a minute later with another detective and sat opposite them.

"Sam," she said, nodding. "Carol. This is detective Brenner, he's assisting on this case." Brenner nodded, but said nothing. "Sam, I'd like you to tell me how you came to be at Mrs. Connors' home, and what you know about her death."

Sam shrugged. "Karen, I know you won't believe this, but I don't know anything about either. I went to see her husband about something to do with one of my investigations, and the next thing I know, I'm waking up beside a dead body. I started to call 911, and then I

heard sirens and cars outside, so I waited, and the door busted open and I was arrested. That is literally all I know."

Brenner snorted, but Parks shushed him. "Sam, are you saying Dr. Connors somehow framed you?"

"That's my belief, yes."

She sat there for a moment, then opened the folder she'd brought in and looked at a page inside it. "Preliminary ballistics says that your gun is the weapon that killed Mrs. Connors."

"I would expect so," Sam said. "Not much point in a frame-up if you don't use the framer's gun."

Parks suppressed a smile. "I was the one who went to tell Dr. Connors that his wife was dead, and that you were found at the scene. He seemed surprised, but I couldn't tell if it was genuine or not. He said you were working for his wife on their divorce, and that you'd been there to see him, said you were offering to get rid of some documentation you'd found on some of his assets in return for a substantial amount of money. He said he told you to get out, you left, and he hadn't been out of the office since then. His dental hygienist and receptionist both confirmed his story, said you stormed out in a huff and that Connors never left the office afterward."

Sam snorted. "That's the kind of story I'd expect him to concoct. Did he suggest a motive, why I might want to kill her? If you check it out, you'll find that I was set to

receive ten percent of the assets she received from him in the divorce, which would have been around sixteen million dollars. Killing her would be like killing that golden goose, wouldn't it?"

She nodded. "I guess so, but he said you were hitting him up for five million, and figures you went there to demand more from her, when you didn't get anywhere with him. If you were after a bigger golden egg, and she didn't cooperate, I can see where things might have gotten heated. One thing leads to another, tempers go through the roof, and a gun goes off. It's happened before."

Sam shook his head. "Karen, you've known me how many years? Have I ever gone off half-cocked?"

"Nope," she said. "But this is the first time we've ever seen this sort of a situation around you, Sam, so we're in unexplored territory. You know how my job works; no matter how I feel about you personally, I've got to look at the evidence, and that doesn't make your armor very shiny right now, old buddy! You got anything you can give me that'll lend any credibility to your story?"

Sam looked at Carol, who shook her head slightly, then turned back to Parks. "How about the fact that Connors stood to lose sixteen million dollars to his wife, which could be a pretty good motive to get rid of her, don't you think?"

"Could be, but he's got a credible alibi, while you were found at the scene with the body and your prints all

over the murder weapon. That makes you the star of the show, Sam, whether any of us likes it or not. On the other hand, if his alibi is false, then that implicates the receptionist and hygienist, as well, as accessories."

Sam sighed. "Karen, do you really believe I did this?"

Parks gave him a sad smile. "Not for a split second, Sam, but it's my job to prove that you did, anyway, and the sad part is that you've given me just about everything I need to do that. If you can give me anything else, anything at all, I'll do what I can, but you gotta give me something to work with."

Sam looked down at the table. "All I can say right now is that there may be something coming. I can't go into it because if you get involved, it could mess up what I'm trying to do."

Brenner had been staring at Parks, but at this, he said, "So, what? You're gonna pull some rabbit out of your hat?"

Parks cut her eyes toward him. "Shut up, Brenner," she said, and then motioned for him to follow her out the door.

Carol patted Sam's hand. "I know it was hard to keep your mouth shut, but I think we need a lot more ammo before we show them our big guns, don't you?"

Sam nodded. "Yeah. I'm okay. At least I know Karen believes I could be innocent, and she's a good cop. That helps."

Carol stood. "Alright, then, I'm going to get on this from every angle I can think of. You keep it together in here." She shook his hand and promised to keep in close touch with both him and Indie. Sam sat there for a few moments after she left, and then the same lady jailer came for him. She looked at him as she walked him back up the hallway.

"I'm hearing rumors that the same demon that got Mr. Morris got hold of you," she said. "I know a couple of cops who know you, and they say there's no way you'd do this, no matter what the evidence looks like."

Sam smiled at her. "Well, you tell them I appreciate it," he said, "but right now, I'm just like Mr. Morris, and I have no real idea exactly what happened. We'll have to wait and see."

She shrugged. "For what it's worth, I think you're innocent." A moment later, she took the cuffs off again as she put him back into the holding cell. He was only there a few seconds before another jailer called him, this time to be booked in on a preliminary charge of first degree murder. He was photographed, fingerprinted, weighed and measured, and then taken to a stall where he was stripped naked and hosed down with something that was supposed to kill head and body lice. After that, he was escorted, still naked, to the showers, where he was given soap and a towel. When his shower was done, he was taken into another room, where he was given the orange jumpsuit that is worn by those charged with felonies.

Sam was officially a prisoner of the Denver detention center.

When he was dressed, he was handed a rolled up mattress, with sheets, a towel and something that was supposed to be a pillow but was about as thick as his living room carpet, and taken into a cell block. He was shown to a cell while other inmates shouted insults and comments about fresh meat. The cell he was taken to held two men, and he saw that the bottom bunk was open, so he made it up for himself and then decided he might as well get it over with. He went out into the day room, and into the cellblock's population of gang bangers, drug dealers, murderers and everyone else.

He saw several faces he knew, people he had once arrested and put in this same facility. The looks they gave him said that they knew him, as well, and a few of them were gathering up and whispering. Sam was looking around, trying to find a spot where he could get his back against a wall, when a hand landed on his shoulder, and he spun, ready to fight—to find Carl Morris smiling at him.

"Hey, Sam," the big man said. "Marilee said you were in here, and told me what happened. I asked her to bunk you in with me, I hope you don't mind. I know your leg is bad, and I moved to the top bunk so you can have the bottom."

Sam swallowed. Just the sight of the big bodybuilder smiling at him was enough to make the others suddenly

want to find something else to do, and Sam could understand why; Carl made Stallone and Schwarzenegger look sort of small.

"Marilee?" Sam asked.

"Yes, she's that little lady jailer who's always so nice. She said she's talked to you a few times, and she likes you. She told me what happened, that it's like what happened to me. Is it really?"

Sam nodded. "Yeah, it is, and maybe more than you can imagine. Carl, I'm pretty sure you are not the person who killed your family. I'm still working on some of the details, but there's a very good chance you may be a free man again one day soon."

Carl looked at him for a moment. "Sam, are you saying someone else killed my wife and kids?" he asked softly.

Sam nodded again. "Yeah, Carl," he said. "It's complicated, but that is exactly what I'm saying. And now we just both have to hope that I can prove it."

Carl stared at him for a moment, then turned and walked over to one of the stainless steel picnic tables that were mounted into the concrete floor and sat on the bench. He leaned his elbows on the table and put his face in his hands, and began to weep.

Sam sat down beside him and put a hand on his shoulder, but didn't say anything while Carl cried his heart out. The sobs got louder and louder, but no one in the room would make a comment, and after a few

moments, everyone there became quiet as the big man wept. Sam heard a rattle and turned to see four of the jailers, including Marilee, standing at the door in silence.

Sam waited until Carl had gotten himself back under control, and then went to the phone on the wall of the day room. It required him to call collect, so he called his house number, rather than Indie's cell.

He gave the automated system his name and waited while it called Indie and asked her if she would accept the call. When she did, he heard her saying, "Hello? Sam? Hello?"

"I'm here, babe," he said. "They got me booked in, and I'm doing okay. How about you?"

She sighed. "Sam, I'm strong," she said, "and I'll do whatever I have to do to help get you out of this mess. I called Mom, and she said Beauregard won't tell her what I'm supposed to do, because he says I have to find the answer on my own, or I won't understand it. And I called Harry; he says he'll try to find out what he can, but he isn't normally allowed any interference in local police matters unless they involve National Security, and this won't. If you've got any ideas..."

"Actually, baby, I do," he said. "I was talking with Carol, the lawyer, and we came up with a game plan. I need you and Herman to go through Connors' patient list and find as many of them as you can. Then, call them and find out if any of them have had any crazy episodes, especially if it involved breaking the law or

getting into trouble. If they've had weird experiences at any time, then check and see if they saw Connors right before it. And, we're particularly looking for any women who have found themselves having sex with him; there were a couple that Carol knew of, but Connors was able to prove that they were the ones who came after him, so the cases never went anywhere."

"Okay, I can do that, and I can get a jump on it; I'll tell Herman to look for any police records that involve his patients right after they saw him, and see if any of them are for strange stuff. Those would stand out like a sore thumb, I think. And I'll check with all of his female patients about the sexual angle. Now, what about Annie and Carl? Is there anything I should be doing about them?"

"No, not at the moment. Al is on his way to go see Annie, and I'm hoping that'll help her memory, and Carl is in here with me. I've let him know that he may not actually be responsible for his family's deaths, and it's hit him pretty hard. Carol will build his defense on what we've got on Connors, if we can get any kind of supporting evidence. We may never get Connors, but we have a good chance of getting acquittals for me and Carl, and I'll take that, for now. Connors I can get another day."

Indie laughed coldly. "Not if I get to him first," she said, but Sam cut her off before she could go any further.

"Indie, don't you go near him! I just went to talk to the man, and look at where I'm at. We can't afford anything happening to you." She was quiet for a moment, and Sam said, "Indie?"

"Okay, okay, I won't go near him. But if he happens to step out in front of the truck, I'm pretty sure I'm gonna have brake failure!"

"Stop it! I mean it, Indie, no! Now, get with Herman and see what you can dig up over the next few days. I'll call you now and then, and we'll compare notes. I love you, baby girl, don't you forget that!"

Indie made a sound that might have been a sob. "I won't," she said, "and don't you, either. I love you, Sam Prichard! And I almost forgot—you've already made the news. Chris and Candy called fifteen minutes ago. I assured them you didn't do it, and they said to let them know when your bail is set."

Sam chuckled. "Okay, babe. Tell 'em I said thanks. I gotta get off here, we only get a few minutes at a time. I'll call you later, before bedtime."

"Okay, Sam. Bye."

"Bye, baby." He hung up, and felt like sitting down to cry himself.

* * * * *

Indie got off the phone with Sam and checked on Kenzie, who was watching TV quietly. She hadn't said much since Indie told her Sam would be gone for a day or two, and Indie guessed that she could sense

something was wrong from her mother's emotional state.

She left the child watching TV, and went to the office to get Herman on the job. She fed him the data she wanted him to search through, and turned him loose on it, then went back to the house to make dinner for herself and her daughter. It seemed like a pizza night, so she popped one into the oven and sat down to watch old Sponge Bob episodes with Kenzie until it was done, and then brought it into the living room on a platter so they could eat it while they watched.

Kenzie looked up at her mother and said, "Is Daddy gonna get shot again?"

Indie did her best to smile. "Nope," she said. "He's just working on a case, and has to be gone for a little while. He'll be home soon, I'm sure."

Kenzie stared at her for a moment, but then she smiled. "I'm glad," she said, "I don't like when he gets shot."

Indie couldn't help laughing, then. "Me, neither!" she said, and Kenzie climbed up to sit beside her on the couch while they ate.

When they'd finished, Indie told Kenzie she had some work to do in the office, and Kenzie opted for a movie. She got into their stash of DVDs and found Despicable Me, one of Kenzie's favorites, and put it in, then went to check on Herman.

The program had been busy. Indie scanned the lines of data on the screen and began clicking the provided

links, one after another.

Many of Connors' patients had experienced minor run-ins with the law, and Herman had cross-referenced them with the dates of their appointments. Several had found themselves in trouble within twenty-four hours after visiting the dentist, and Indie started going through the various cases.

Robert Morgan, seventeen: The night after his tooth was pulled, he was arrested for indecent exposure, while taking a leak at nine PM on his front lawn. Several neighbors were out on the street, and when one of them asked him why he was doing it, he asked, "Why, don't you?" Later, he told police that he had no memory of the event at all.

Susan Bergen, twenty-four: The night after she went in for a filling, she was arrested for driving through town with no clothes on. According to the arresting officers, she seemed dazed, and thought the arrest was funny. She woke up several hours later with no idea how she'd gotten to jail, and no memory of anything from the night before.

Donald Miller, fifty-six: Early in the morning after a late afternoon appointment to get three teeth extracted, neighbors called police when they saw him in his driveway, hacking his own dog to pieces with an ax. A few hours later, he broke down while in police custody after they had to tell him what he'd done. The dog had been a beloved pet of his wife, who had passed away a

year earlier, and neighbors said they couldn't believe he'd done it because he treated the dog as if it were a child.

Nathan Sparks, eighteen: The night after he got a tooth filled, he reportedly asked three teenaged girls to strip naked on top of his car, while he drove through town. He was not arrested, but was warned against making any further such requests. His parents later filed a lawsuit against police that alleged they had made the whole thing up, since their son couldn't remember anything about it at all, but it was dismissed when the entire police report was shown to them, including recordings of their son laughing and telling police that if they had waited a few more minutes, they would have gotten a free show.

Kate Milligan, nineteen: Kate had two teeth filled, and later that night was arrested at the home of Dr. Connors, where she was standing on his wife's car and calling for him to come and have sex with her. She woke up in jail, completely unaware of what had transpired.

Alan Batts, thirty-four: The night after an extraction, he had gone to bed with his wife, but she said he got up an hour later and said he wanted something to eat. He seemed out of sorts, she had said, so when he was gone downstairs for more than half an hour, she went down to see if he was okay, and found him eating their children's pet mice. He was popping them into his mouth and chewing them up, she said, as if they were pizza rolls. When she tried to make him stop, he accused her of trying to steal them from him and threatened to kill her,

so she called police, who took him to a mental facility. The next morning, he couldn't remember a thing, but complained of pain in his mouth, where the mice had apparently scratched and bitten his tongue many times.

Darren Pickford, sixty: The night after he got his last seven teeth pulled, in preparation for new dentures, he went to bed as usual, according to his wife, but then rose around 2 a.m. She thought he'd gone to the bathroom, but a few minutes later she saw flashing lights outside her window and looked out to see two officers wrestling her husband to the ground. She ran outside to find that he was being arrested for aiming a gun at people in cars driving by, and his shotgun was lying on the ground beside him. Like all of the others, when he awoke the next morning in jail, he couldn't remember any of it, and refused to believe he'd actually done it until he saw dash cam video from the police car.

And then she hit the one that made her skin crawl.

Betty Morgenstern, twenty: Late in the night after having three teeth pulled, neighbors found her in the bedroom of their twelve-year old twin boys, attempting to instruct them in the arts of sex. She was arrested and taken to jail, but woke up several hours later unable to remember what had happened or how she'd come to be in jail. When she learned what she had done, she went back into her cell, took off her jumpsuit and hung herself. She was seen by a jailer, who tried to save her, but it was too late. Betty had been a student at a theological seminary school, and had planned to become

a missionary.

Indie read through several more such cases, including five more that resulted in suicides, and compiled a report that she emailed to Carol Spencer. She added a note that she planned to contact as many of them as she could the next morning.

Sam called just as she was finishing up, and she glanced out the window to see that it was dark. She waited for the recording to tell her to press five, then pushed the button.

"Hey, babe," she said. "I won't waste our time with the details, but I've got a couple dozen cases of people getting into legal trouble after appointments with Alex Connors. Some of the stories are almost funny, but some of them are just tragic. Six people who got messed up after seeing him have killed themselves, including one girl who only had sex with him, and couldn't live with the things people were saying about her."

Sam sighed. "I can't say I'm surprised. If I didn't know what was going on, this might be more than I could handle. See if you can talk to any of them, and get them to remember the connection, but be careful. We don't know whether any of these folks might be friends of his, and I don't want him to know what you're doing."

"I'll be careful," she said. "How is it in there?"

Sam laughed. "Well, there are half a dozen of my old arrests from vice in here, and I'm sure they'd love to beat me to death, but Carl is my cellmate, and he makes the

Incredible Hulk look tiny. About the time they realized that he liked me, they all decided to let bygones be bygones. Carl saw how they were looking at me a bit ago, and walked over and said something to them, I don't know what, but a couple of them have even offered me soda pop and candy bars!"

"Yikes, don't take any! You never know what might be in them!"

"Don't worry, baby, I won't. Indie, thank you for what you're doing. I know this isn't the kind of thing you're used to, but..."

"Sam, stop," she said. "I'm not doing anything more than any other woman would do to save her man. I just happen to have the right skills and resources, is all. I can do this, honey, I can. And Kenzie sends her love, by the way."

"You tell her I love her too, and can't wait to see here when I get home. Does she know that might be a while?"

Indie gave a sigh. "I told her you're gone on work, and we don't know how long, yet, but that you'll be home as soon as you can. She's okay with that, she says, as long as you're not gonna get shot again."

Sam laughed again. "Tell her I agree with that, completely. I love you, babe, but I gotta go, there are others who want to use the phone."

"Okay," she said, but then, "hey, wait! Is Carl there with you? Can I talk to him?"

"Um, yeah," Sam said, "just a sec."

A moment later, a deep, cultured voice came on the line. "Hello?"

"Hi, Carl, this is Indie, Sam's wife. I just wanted to say thanks for watching out for him in there."

She could hear the big man's smile. "It's my pleasure, Miss Indie," he said. "He tells me you're the one who's working on proving we aren't as bad as they say we are, so I want to thank you, too."

"Believe me, Carl, it's my pleasure," she said, and then Sam came back on.

"Babe? I gotta go, I love you!"

"I love you too, Sam, I love you!"

The line went dead, and Indie sat there for a moment holding the phone to her ear. She finally hung it up, and then sat back and let the tears flow. A few moments later, she broke down and called her mother and told her everything.

7

Indie woke at seven the next morning and got Kenzie up and ready for an adventure. She had called Anita Mitchell, the neighbor whose twins Kenzie often played with, the night before and arranged for Kenzie to spend the day with them. Kenzie was excited about it, because it would be the first time she'd gotten to see them in a few weeks; during Sam and Indie's honeymoon, she had stayed with her two grandmothers, who lived out in Aurora, and hadn't had the chance to go and play since they'd gotten back. Since Jim and Anita didn't mind, even Samson got to go along, so Indie would have the whole day free to start working on the case.

She dropped kid and cat off about eight, and headed back to the house to get started. Her plan was to first try calling each of the people who had been affected and see if they would be willing to cooperate, holding out the incentive that they might get their records expunged if it

could be established that they were not in any way responsible for their actions. She sat down at Sam's desk and started going through the list.

Herman had managed to identify and get numbers for most of them the night before, and she had the list printed out in front of her. She gathered her courage and dialed the first number: Susan Bergen.

"Hello?" came a sleepy voice.

"Hi, is this Susan Bergen?" Indie asked.

"Um—who's calling, please?"

"My name is Indiana Prichard, and I work with my husband Sam, who's a private investigator. We're working on a case involving some people who have had some bizarre behavioral episodes after a dental treatment, and your name came up as a possible victim."

"Dental treatment? I'm not sure I understand..."

"Susan, you were arrested for driving nude the night after you had a cavity filled. You said you had no idea why you were doing it and didn't even remember it afterward, right?"

"Um—yeah, that's right. Are you saying it was because of the filling?"

"Not the filling, but other people who have gone to the same dentist for different treatments have had similar incidents, although some of them had far worse consequences. Do you remember going to get a filling that morning?"

The woman was quiet for a moment, then said, "Well—not really. I mean, I remember being arrested, well, not being arrested, but waking up and finding out I'd been arrested. The whole thing seems like a nightmare, now, to be honest. I got two years of probation over it, and I'd never been in trouble in my life before that."

"I know, right? The thing is, if we can prove that these weird episodes are related to that dentist, then it's quite possible that this could be removed from your record. Would you be willing to testify about what happened to you?"

"I—I guess so, but I can't even remember whether I went to the dentist that morning. How could we prove that?"

"That's no problem," Indie said. "I've got the dentist's appointment calendar for the past five years, and it shows that you were there that very morning. Listen, I'm going to have an attorney contact you, okay? She'll be able to explain more about this, and how you can hopefully get your record cleaned up again."

"Okay, sure," Susan said, obviously getting excited about the prospect of clearing her record.

Indie thanked her, and made a note that she had her first cooperative witness, then she dialed the next number on her list.

"Hi, is this Donald Miller?" she said as soon as the man answered.

"Yes, can I help you?"

"Mr. Miller, my name is Indiana Prichard, and I work for my husband Sam, who's a private investigator. We're looking into a case involving people who have had strange episodes they can't explain after a dental treatment, and your name is on the list, because of what happened last year with your dog. It's very likely, sir, that you were not responsible for that incident, because you had three teeth pulled the evening before, and what happened is almost certainly a side effect of the treatment you received."

Miller was quiet for a few seconds, and then asked, "Do you mean you might be able to explain this to me? Tell me why I did this horrible thing?"

"Mr. Miller," she said, "a lot of people who went to see Dr. Connors have had bizarre episodes like yours, some of them with a lot worse end consequences. What we're trying to do is show that there is a pattern, here, that people who have gone to his office for treatments tend to then do things that are completely out of character for them. We believe that he's doing something there that is causing this, and that he knows it. One man who went there a few weeks ago is in jail right now for murdering his own family, and he has no idea what happened, just like you didn't know until you were told."

"Young lady, if this is true, then I might finally be able to forgive myself," he said sadly. "How can I be of

help to you in this?"

"Sir, what I'm hoping is that you'll be willing to testify about what you went through. We can show for certain that it happened after the dental appointment, just like all the other people I'm talking to, so if you would..."

"Of course I will," he said. "I've gone to Dr. Connors for a long time, but if he's doing something like this—of course I'll help."

Indie pumped the air with her fist, and put a check by his name. "That's great, sir. I'm going to have an attorney get in touch, okay, to go over all of this with you. She should be calling soon."

"That'll be fine, dear," he said. Indie thanked him again and moved to the next call.

"Hello?"

"Hello, Mr., Sparks? My name is Indiana..." She went through her spiel, but this time she got a resounding "no!" Nathan Sparks only wanted to put the incident behind him, and wasn't interested in any explanations for why he'd done what he'd done. He hadn't gotten into any serious trouble, and just wanted to forget the whole thing ever happened.

She called Robert Morgan next, explained who she was and the reason for her call, and he was delighted to learn that there was a probable reason for his behavior that night. He agreed to testify, and wanted to know how soon he could expect to do so. Indie said she didn't know, but that she'd have the attorney call as soon as

possible.

Alan Batts agreed to testify. His wife had left him after the incident with the mice, afraid that he might one night become dangerous. They'd been talking about reconciliation, though, and he hoped that this might be the impetus she needed to bring her back home.

Kate Milligan also agreed. She'd often wondered if Dr. Connors had somehow manipulated her into what had happened that night, because she always felt that he was ogling her whenever she had to go to his office, even when she was barely in her teens.

"I'd love to see him nailed for this, if he's really doing it," she said. "Listen, can I tell you something?"

"Sure," Indie said, suddenly curious. "Anything."

"Well, no one knows this, and if it comes out, well, it might upset my folks—but that wasn't the only time something weird happened. When I was only fifteen, I went to bed one night, and when I woke up, I was naked and in a park, and I could tell I'd—well, had sex. I didn't remember anything about it, though, so I just looked around and found my clothes, then went home and never said anything, but I can tell you it was the night after I got a couple of teeth pulled. I remember that because I'm a bit of a bleeder, and I still had some gauze in my mouth when I woke up. If you need me to, I could tell about that, too."

"I'll let you talk to the attorney about it, okay? I think she'd be the one to discuss that with."

Darren Pickford was happy to help. The incident had gotten him a felony conviction for unlawful use of a firearm, and he'd lost his right to even own a gun. He'd been an avid hunter, and would do anything to get his record expunged and get his second amendment rights restored to him.

Indie spoke to a woman named Julia Stoner who had gone in for an extraction and ended up that night in jail for prostitution, with two uniformed police officers claiming she offered them sex in exchange for money. Julia was the wife of a pastor at a small church, and the incident had destroyed both the church and her marriage. She was delighted to find out that there might be a reason other than demonic possession for her behavior, and would be more than happy to testify.

David Lancer had gone to see Dr. Connors for fillings, and had been picked up that night at the zoo, trying to climb into the lion enclosure. He insisted to the officers that the lion had insulted him, and he was planning to kick its butt as a lesson not to talk that way to humans! He had been in a high security job, but after that incident, he had lost his security clearance and his position. He was also glad to help.

Jillian Butler declined. She had a procedure at the office, but had later been caught breaking into a bakery to steal doughnuts. She had a bag with about eighty of them when police responded to the broken window alarm. She'd managed to avoid jail time and just wanted to live the incident down.

By noon, Indie had twenty-seven people who were willing to testify that they suffered bizarre behavioral episodes after being seen by Dr. Connors. She sent the list of to Carol Spencer, then called her to let her know she'd sent it. The lawyer was ecstatic that she'd had such success, and said she'd get to work setting up depositions immediately. That would be the first step, she explained in getting the prosecutor to pay attention when they asked to have Connors detained.

"Detained?" Indie asked. "Don't we have to prove he was doing it deliberately to do that?"

"Oh, not at all," Carol said. "All we have to show is that there is a definite connection between his treatments and these episodes. We can't prove that any drugs or alcohol were involved in these older cases, and without being able to show that as part of the pattern, we can't really prove that he had any knowledge of the effects, but that doesn't mean he isn't culpable. We can ask for his detention based on the likelihood that he might flee if he isn't held, in order to avoid the civil liability when all of these people file lawsuits against him. There is a lot of precedent for that type of detention, and I plan to go after it hot and heavy!"

Sam called at lunchtime, and was delighted when Indie told him how many she'd gotten and what the lawyer had said. "Baby, you're the best," he said. "We've just had lunch here, and let me tell you that there isn't anyone here who can cook like you can, but it was filling. Carl says hi, and I've gotta say that he's like a new man.

He still feels awful about what happened, but if we can show that it wasn't the real him doing it, I think he'll make it through this. I just hope we can get him acquitted."

"We will, Sam, and you, too! Connors isn't going to get away with this, I won't stand for it!"

They chatted a bit more, and Indie told him that she was going to work on finding even more of Connors' victims, by simply calling patients cold and asking if they'd ever had such episodes. He told her she was dynamite, and she laughed.

"Yeah, and you know about dynamite, right? It comes in small packages!"

They said their I-love-yous, and hung up. Indie went to the kitchen to make herself something for lunch, decided on leftover pizza from the night before, and was just putting it into the microwave when her cell phone rang. It was Sam's mother's number, and she cringed as she answered.

"Hello, Grace," she said, and that was as far as she got.

"Indie! Oh, my God, you've got to talk to your mother, I don't know what to do! Beauregard has her convinced she's a superwoman, and she won't listen to me, here, I'm putting her on the phone!" Indie heard a rustling, and her mother's voice saying, "Now, you know it's just going to upset her," and then her mom came on the line.

"Hi, Sweetie," she said cheerfully.

"Mom," Indie said, "what in the world are you up to?"

"Oh, it's really not that big a deal," her mother, whose name was Kim, said. "I told Grace she shouldn't call you, but you know how she is, always worrying."

"Mom, just cut the crap and tell me what's going on, now."

Kim sighed. "Well, I was talking this whole mess over with Beauregard, and he suggested I go and see that dentist, you know, get a treatment. If he's really using this thing of his to get women, well, I'm still an attractive little tart, everyone says so, and I thought maybe he'd try it on me."

Indie had to admit that she was right about that; at forty-three, Kim was often mistaken for a girl in her early to mid twenties, but that didn't mean this idea wasn't insane.

"Mom, are you *crazy?*" Indie demanded. "This man is dangerous, Mom, just look what he did to Sam!"

"I know, I know, but Beauregard says we can handle this, that he can keep me from doing anything stupid or weird, and what we'd do, you see, is go right after I left and get my blood tested, see if he used any of his drugs on me. That's all it would take, you know, and then you'd have proof that he uses it on people."

"Mom..."

"Beauregard says it's perfectly safe, since he can stop

me from doing anything even if that man tells me to," Kim went on, "and if we did find those drugs in my blood, then we'd have something you and your lawyer can use, right?"

Indie hated to admit it, but that part at least sounded like it could be sensible. As for Beauregard being able to keep Kim from acting stupid, Indie wasn't so sure; her mother could act pretty strange even without any mind altering substances in her system! "Mom, I really don't think..."

"Indiana, my mind is made up. I already called and made an appointment, and I really do have a tooth that needs filling. I've been putting it off for a while, so if he does nothing else, maybe I can at least get it filled and it'll stop keeping me awake at night, and Beauregard says we can even come over tonight and let you keep me handcuffed to something, so I can't go out and do anything, although he says that won't happen anyway, because he can keep me from doing anything like that."

Indie sighed. She knew there was no way she could stop her mother when she—and Beauregard—decided to do something. "Okay, fine, you can go, but I'm going with you. What time is your appointment?"

"It's at three," Kim said. "I can meet you there, or do you want me to come to your house?"

"Come to the house," Indie said firmly. "I'm not having you out driving around with God knows what in your system, so I'll drive!"

"Okay, honey, I'll be there in a bit." She hung up, and Indie sat down and kicked herself for agreeing to this mad plan.

Still, her mother was right about one thing; if she came away from the appointment with zolpidem, or any other drugs, in her blood, then it was more evidence that Connors was guilty. She thought about it for a moment, and then slapped her forehead.

The presence of drugs in her mother's blood after the visit wouldn't necessarily prove that they could only have gotten there at the dental office. For that, they'd need a control test. She grabbed her phone and called Carol Spencer, explaining what her mother wanted to do.

"I think it's brilliant," the lawyer said, "but you're right, we need a blood sample from before, as well. Can you run her by a lab, if I get it set up, so they can get a control sample of her blood before the appointment?"

"Yes, just tell me where and let them know that we'll probably be in a hurry!"

"I'll call you back in five minutes," Carol said, and hung up.

She actually called back in two. "Okay, the lab is only a half mile from Connors' office, so you can go straight to the appointment afterward. I told them to draw a control sample and start the analysis as soon as they do, so that we can get the results quickly. Then, take her right back afterward, and they'll get the comparison

sample. This could actually be the break we need, Indie, and you tell your mother I applaud her courage!"

Indie sighed. "It isn't courage," she said, "it's Beauregard. And no, I won't explain that right now, but we'll get the blood samples."

Her mother showed up at two, and Indie explained about the need for a control blood sample. Kim smiled and agreed, and they got into the truck and headed out. It was about a twenty-minute drive to the lab, and they got there at just before two-thirty. The phlebotomist was ready and waiting when they arrived, and took them right into the back to draw the sample. They took a full vial of blood, and put a drop of Dermabond—also known as medical superglue—on it to stop the bleeding when they were done.

Kim said, "Well, look at that, they don't even use Band-Aids anymore," and Indie hurried her out the door. They drove to the dental clinic, and walked in ten minutes before Kim's appointment.

The blonde receptionist looked up as they entered. "Hi, and welcome to Connors Dental. How can we help you today?"

Kim smiled, and Indie grinned. If there was one thing Indie knew her mom could do, it was act!

"Hello," Kim said. "I've got an appointment to have a cavity looked at. Kim Perkins is my name."

The receptionist smiled. "Oh, yes, I remember. You were lucky we had an opening, but we had a cancellation

this morning, so I was able to get you in." She handed Kim a clipboard and a pen. "If you'll just fill this out, please," she said, and Kim took it and went to a chair near the outer wall to do so, with Indie right behind her.

Indie sat quietly while her mom filled out the questionnaire, providing accurate information about allergies, previous procedures and such, but avoiding the truth on her age (she put down twenty-seven) and address. When she was done, she handed it back to the receptionist and sat down again to wait.

They didn't wait long. Another patient came out, and then a hygienist called for Kim. She patted Indie's hand and told her to just wait there, then smiled and followed the girl into the back.

Indie waited, and then waited some more. She was just about to ask the receptionist how much longer it would be when Kim came out. She looked at Indie and said, her words slightly slurred, "All done. My tongue is a li'l bit numb, so if I sound funny, dat's why." Her eyes seemed okay, though, so Indie smiled and they went out to the truck.

"So," Indie asked when they got inside. "Anything weird happen?"

"Well," Kim said, her speech still a bit slurred, "I don't think so, but I was hypnotized, so I don't really remember anything. He said he still uses Novocaine because it stops pain afterward, but when I was under the hypnosis, I didn't feel a thing. I don't remember anything

at all."

"Okay, well, let's go get your blood drawn again. The sooner we know if you got anything extra in there, the better I'll feel!"

They went right back to the lab, and the same phlebotomist drew a second vial of blood. This time she used a Band-Aid to staunch the bleeding, one with purple and pink hearts on it. Kim smiled, and said, "Oh, look how cute!" Indie hustled her out the door again, and they went back to the house.

Kim wanted to go home, but Indie wasn't having it. "Oh, no, you're staying right here 'til I know you're okay! Some of the people who were affected didn't show any sign of it until the next day, so you're not getting out of my sight until tomorrow night!"

"But, honey, Beauregard says..."

"I don't give a hoot what Beauregard says, this time it's what I say! You're staying right here, and I'm not taking my eyes off you till I know you're okay!"

* * * * *

At four o'clock, Sam heard his name called and looked up to see the jailer, Marilee, at the cellblock door. He went to her, and she held out a pair of cuffs. "You've got a visit, your lawyer," she said, and Sam turned his back obediently.

She led him down the hallways to the interview room, where Carol was waiting. The look on her face didn't make Sam happy, but he waited until Marilee was

gone before he looked at her and said, "Well?"

"I got the blood report back, Sam," she said sadly. "There was no zolpidem in your system, and no alcohol. They did find, however," and her face suddenly brightened, "that you had recently had a fairly high anesthetic dose of ketamine! If you don't know, ketamine is normally used in anesthesia, and works very quickly. If you were given an injection of it, you'd be out of it pretty quickly, and wouldn't remember the injection or any struggle that may have occurred before you went under. Got any sore spots where a needle might have gotten you?"

Sam stared. "Not that I've noticed. What about hypnotic effects? Could it have been used to make me kill someone?"

"Doubtful," Carol said excitedly, and Sam stared even harder. "On the dosage they found in your system, buddy, I don't think you could have even walked out of that place! You probably would have had to have been carried out, and if I'm right, then there's no way you could have killed Juliette Connors! Someone else would have had to carry you there, and that means someone else would have had to fire the fatal shot. If I can get that through a few prosecutorial heads, then by this time tomorrow, I'll have you out of here, and all charges dismissed!"

Sam sat there, frozen. "Carol," he said finally, "are you sure?"

"Well, I can't be a hundred percent certain, of course, but I think there's a very good chance. The only thing that worries me is that this hurts our defense for Carl, but if your mother-in-law has any luck..."

Sam's eyes shot wide open. "My mother in law? What's Kim got to do with this?"

Carol looked at him. "Uh-oh, did I let a cat out of the bag? I thought you would have known; she made an appointment with Dr. Connors today, and went and got her blood tested both before and after. We're praying he used the zolpidem on her, because then we can tie him to it directly!"

Sam stared at her. "That idiot!" he said suddenly. "She has no clue what she's sticking her nose into! How could she be so stupid?"

Carol looked at him in surprise. "Sam, I'm confused," she said. "This woman just put herself on the line to try to prove you were innocent. Frankly, I think she's amazingly brave!"

"She isn't brave, she's psychotic! Somehow I just know that stupid Beauregard is behind this!"

"Hey, your wife said almost the same thing. Who on earth is Beauregard?"

"Nobody!" Sam yelled, and then refused to say another word on the subject.

As soon as he got back to the cellblock, Sam went to the phones and called home. When Indie answered, he said, "Would someone please tell me how to kill that

ghost?"

"Uh-oh," Indie said. "Carol must have come to see you."

"Yeah, and she told me about this harebrained scheme of your mother's to go get doped up by Dr. Demento! It was Beauregard, wasn't it? Did she say this was his idea?"

"Well, yes, but..."

"Baby, how could you have let her go through with this? Where is she now? Locked up somewhere safe, I hope?"

"Um—she's in the living room, watching TV. But, Sam, before you go all nuts on me, don't worry, I handcuffed her to the gas pipe on the fireplace. She can't possibly get out of it, and I'm going to stay up all night and watch her. And Kenzie is staying with the twins tonight, Anita said it was no problem."

Sam counted to ten, then said, "Okay. Fine, it's already done and there's no undoing it. Meanwhile, back at the ranch, Carol came to tell me that the blood test shows there was no zolpidem in my system. Instead, they found ketamine, which probably knocked me out to the point that I couldn't possibly have killed Mrs. Connors. It looks like I was just plain framed, and she's gonna try to convince the prosecutor of that in the morning and get me released, but that's not definite. We still need to nail Connors, if we can, and use that to show malice. If we can establish that he uses drugs to manipulate people,

then we can probably show that he had the only viable motive to kill his wife, and thought he could shut me up in the process."

"We're working on it," Indie said. "Carol's got depositions set for tomorrow with a lot of the witnesses I found, and that will help. If it turns out Mom got a dose of zolpidem, then we've probably got enough to hang him, and that's what I'm hoping for. That should give us enough to show you were framed, too."

Sam sighed. "Yeah," he said. "Baby, I'm sorry I yelled at you. I just got worried when she said your mom tried this. If he'd known she was connected to me, she could be dead by now."

"I know, Sam, but she was really just trying to help. And Beauregard, figment of her mind though he is, does have a tendency to be right. This could work; if he really uses his tricks to hook up with women, well, Mom's not bad looking, and she passes for my sister all the time. He might go for her, and then we'll have proof."

"Okay, baby. I love you, and I'll try to call you back later tonight. Keep a close eye on her, don't let her do anything stupid."

"Trust me on that, babe," she said. "She isn't getting out of my sight!"

8

Indie heated up frozen sandwiches for herself and Kim, and they sat in the living room to eat and watch a movie. They had looked through what was on, and finally settled on one of the latest superhero movies. Kim enjoyed them, and Indie liked the action. When it was over, they sat and talked for a bit, and Kim drifted off to sleep on the couch.

Indie hadn't lied to Sam about cuffing her mother to the gas pipe, but she'd actually hooked several pairs of Sam's cuffs together and made a chain about three feet long, with the other end of it hooked to her mother's ankle. Kim couldn't move more than few feet away from the couch, but it allowed her to stretch out and lay down. She was sleeping peacefully, while Indie sat there and watched a movie called "Fireproof," about a fireman who was having problems in his marriage, and embarked on a forty-day challenge to try to win back his wife's love

and respect. It was a wonderful movie, and she found herself in tears at the end.

Kim was still sleeping, and Indie saw that it was nearly eleven. She flipped channels and tried to find another movie, but finally gave up. She went to the bookshelf beside the fireplace and looked through the books; she'd always enjoyed reading, and hadn't had much time, lately. This seemed like a good chance to renew the hobby. She found a book of Sam's called "The Very Swift Witches," and the title caught her eye, so she flipped it over and read the back. It was a comic drama about three witches from seventeenth century Wales who are magically transported to the Ozark Mountains of today, adopted by a single mother and her kids, and have to adapt to a world where magic is unknown, and carriages run around without any horses to pull them! It sounded cute, so she took it back to the recliner and began to read.

Two hours later, after stifling laughter several times and even shedding a few tears, she glanced up to see her mother sitting straight up on the couch, with her eyes wide open.

"Mom?" she said. Kim looked at her for a second, but then seemed to ignore her again. She looked down at her purse and reached for it, digging in the bottom of it for something, and then came up with a small bottle. She unscrewed the cap and started to put it to her mouth, but then stopped suddenly.

Her face turned to Indie, who was already on her feet and moving toward her mother. She said, "I think perhaps you should take this bottle from your mother, Indiana," but the voice that came out of her wasn't her own. It had a distinct masculine quality, and Indie froze where she stood.

"Mom?" she said again, and her mother's face smiled while she shook her head.

"I'm afraid she's not here, at the moment, Indiana. She is somewhere in her mind, and I've had to take over to keep anything from happening."

Indie stared. "B—Beauregard?" she asked, and her mother nodded.

"Yes, dear girl," that odd voice said. "Now, please—take the bottle. It may contain something dangerous."

Indie reached out and took the bottle, then got the cap from her mother's other hand. She carefully put it back on, and then looked at her mother again.

"Is Mom okay?" she asked.

"She is acting on something she was told earlier," the voice said. "She wants to drink that bottle, and then go to a place to meet that fool dentist."

Indie stared for another minute. "And you're Beauregard? Are you real? Really a ghost, I mean?"

Her mother's face smiled, a jovial expression that was so unlike the way Kim normally looked that it sent a chill down Indie's spine. "I certainly think so, though I know that others don't believe it. Sometimes your mother

doesn't believe it, but she still listens to me. She's ready to go back to sleep, now, I think."

A moment later, Kim lay back down, and Indie stood there until she heard her mother's breathing become deep and steady once again. She looked at the bottle in her hand, and then took it to the kitchen and hid it in the back of a cabinet. She made a pot of coffee while she was there, and waited until there was enough to pour herself a cup.

When she got back to the living room, she half expected to see Kim sitting up again, but she was still sleeping peacefully. Indie watched her for a few more moments, and then picked up her book again and sat down to read. She looked up every few minutes to check on her mother, but Kim didn't move again the rest of the night. Indie didn't take any chances, though, and between the coffee and the book, she managed to remain awake with no problem.

In the morning, Kim awakened normally, stretched and yawned and smiled at her daughter. "See? Everything was fine. I'm still here, and nothing happened in the night."

Indie stared at her for a moment. "Mom," she said at last, "you don't remember anything from last night?"

Kim looked at her, and frowned. "No. Should I?"

Indie sat there for a moment, then said, "Last night, about one, you sat up and got a small bottle out of your purse. You were about to drink it, but then you stopped,

and..." She trailed off, and had to force herself to go on. "And then you looked at me and said I should take it, but it didn't sound like you, and when I asked if you were okay, you said you were Beauregard. You—he said you were gone in your mind somewhere, and that you were trying to do what Dr. Connors told you to do, to drink whatever's in that bottle and then go to see him, but he stopped you."

Kim smiled. "Ah," she said, "so you finally got to talk to him. He doesn't come out very often, he says he doesn't like it out here." She cocked her head as if listening for a moment, then smiled at Indie again. "He says to tell you that he doesn't always believe in himself, either, whatever that means."

Indie shook her head, and another chill went down her spine. "Listen, I need to take that bottle to the lawyer so she can get it checked out. Do you need to go to the bathroom or anything?"

Kim laughed. "Well, yes, I could stand to. Would you mind?"

Indie unlocked the cuff on her ankle and followed her to the bathroom, waiting outside while her mother took care of necessary things. When she came out, they went back to the couch and Indie hooked her ankle back up again.

"Sorry, Mom, but I'm not letting you go until I know you're clean."

Kim smiled. "I understand, honey, don't worry. I'll

be fine, but could I have some of that coffee?"

Indie got her a cup, made the way she liked it, and gave her the remote and the book. "If you get sick of the TV, try this. I read it last night, and it's pretty good."

Kim glanced at the back and said, "Ooh, witches! It sounds good!" She giggled like a teenager, and Indie rolled her eyes.

She went into the kitchen and got the bottle out of the cabinet. Curiosity got the better of her, and she opened the cap and sniffed at it, but jerked back instantly. It smelled like some pretty potent alcohol, stronger than anything Indie had ever tried, and she put the cap back on quickly. She would bet that the zolpidem they were looking for was in that bottle.

She called Carol at eight, and her secretary answered.

"Hi, this is Indiana Prichard," she said. "I've got something that Carol needs to see right away. Is she in?"

"Actually, she is, but she's in a deposition already this morning. She should be free in about an hour, if you'd like to come then?"

Indie smiled. "I'll be there," she said, and went to take a shower and get dressed.

When she came out, she checked on her mother and found her reading contentedly. Kim glanced up at her and waved with her fingers, and Indie rolled her eyes again. She grabbed the bottle and headed out the door, telling Kim she'd be back as soon as she could. She went out to the truck and got in, started it up and drove off

toward Carol's office downtown.

She arrived at the office as Carol was finishing up with Donald Miller, the old man who had butchered his dog after visiting Dr. Connors a year before. He was smiling, but there were traces of tears on his face as he left, and Indie was surprised to see that Carol's cheeks were also damp.

"That poor man has been beating himself up for a year because of what happened," Carol said. "Now he has a chance to find peace, knowing that it wasn't just some suppressed insanity of his own that made him do it. We're not only going to nail Connors, Indie, we're helping people recover their lives." She wiped her eyes quickly. "Now, you've got something for me?"

Indie produced the bottle. "I took this from my mom about one o'clock this morning," she said. "She sat up suddenly from a deep sleep, dug it out of her purse and was going to drink it, but I managed to take it away. She mumbled something about drinking it, then going to see Dr. Connors someplace." Indie had decided that she didn't want to even try to explain Beauregard.

Carol looked at the bottle. "Has it been out of your control since you took it from your mother?" she asked.

Indie shook her head in the negative. "No, I hid it in a cabinet and didn't take it out until this morning. There was no one else in the house, and I was awake all night, so no one could have tampered with it."

"Okay, good, so we've got a simple chain of custody.

I want you to take it over to the same lab you went to yesterday; I'll call and tell them what to do with it. You get a receipt from whoever you hand it to, and bring that back to me, okay?"

Indie agreed, and left. She took the bottle to the lab, where a chemist gave her a signed receipt, and took that straight back to Carol. Once she handed it over, she went home again, and found her mother sitting there with tears in her eyes.

"Mom? What's wrong?" she asked, but Kim only shook her head as she wiped at her eyes.

"I'm okay," she said. "I just finished the book, and the ending made me cry."

Indie stared at her. "You read that book in two hours? It took me all night!"

Kim waved it off. "Speed reading course, two years ago, before you came back from college. It was great, you should try it."

Indie rolled her eyes. "I don't have that much time for reading," she said.

"You would if you took the course," Kim replied. "I usually read at least one book a day, now. It's very relaxing."

"I'll bet. You need the bathroom or anything?"

Kim shook her head. "No, not right now. But I could use another cup of coffee."

Indie went to get it for her, and was bringing it back

when her phone rang. It was Carol Spencer.

"Hello?" Indie said.

"Indie, we're looking good! The lab says the bottle you brought in contained four ounces of pure, two hundred proof grain alcohol with ten milligrams of zolpidem tartrate dissolved in it. I've been thinking about our next step, and I'd like your mother to be seen by another hypnotist. I've talked to a psychiatrist who is very knowledgeable and is willing to see her right away. What I'm hoping is that he can actually recover what posthypnotic suggestions she was given, so we can get right down to what Connors was up to. Can you get here there in the next hour or so?"

"Sure," Indie said. "Gimme the address."

"Great! It's Dr. Annalee Stratton, and she's over at one thousand Greenbriar Avenue. She's expecting you any time, so just go on over as soon as you can."

"You got it!" Indie hung up the phone and said, "Mom, I'll make this to go. You're finally going to see a shrink!"

Kim smiled. "Oh, how exciting!"

Indie rolled her eyes once again, but found a travel cup for her mom's coffee, then made another one for herself. They left the house a few minutes later, after a stop in the bathroom for each of them, and arrived at Dr. Stratton's office after a thirty-minute drive.

The receptionist there was thin and brunette, and ushered them right into the doctor's office as soon as she

got Kim's name. She had Kim sit in a recliner, and offered Indie a straight-backed chair, then left. Dr. Stratton came in a moment later, a lovely woman who reminded Indie of one of old porcelain dolls from the early twentieth century. Indie introduced them.

"Hi," she said, "I'm Dr. Stratton. Ms. Spencer has given me a pretty clear description of the situation, and I'll be honest and tell you that I'm appalled that any medical professional would abuse the power of his position this way. We'll be placing you under hypnotic induction, into the 'trance state,' as it's called. In this state, we should be able to direct you to recall things that you were instructed to forget or conceal, and remove that injunction so that you can tell us about them. Is that okay with you?"

Kim smiled. "Yes, certainly. I understand I tried to do some strange things last night, and I'd love to know what it was I was trying to do. Right now, I can't remember anything."

Dr. Stratton nodded. "That's because you were instructed not to remember when you're awake. Let's begin, then, shall we? What I want you to do is get yourself as comfortable in the chair as you can, and then we're going to begin."

Indie held up a hand. "Should I leave the room? I mean, I don't need to be hypnotized..."

Dr. Stratton smiled. "You can stay if you wish. What we're going to do is directed at your mother, and

shouldn't affect you at all. You may find yourself relaxing, but you'll be in control of yourself at all times, both of you. All we're really doing is guiding your mother into a relaxation technique that will remove some of her inhibitions, especially any artificial ones from the dentist. Ready?"

Kim nodded with a smile, and Dr. Stratton began speaking softly.

"What I want you to do is simply relax and listen to my voice. You're sitting comfortably and relaxing, and that's all you need to be doing right now..."

Indie watched, fascinated, as her mother's face relaxed completely. Kim usually wore a slight smile, as if life were a joke that she alone could understand, but even that little smile slowly faded away as she listened to the doctor speaking in a soft monotone.

"...feeling like you're sort of floating, you can't even feel the chair under you. Your mind is relaxed, and relaxation is good, oranges are good, too, and sometimes you can find yourself riding in an orange car, riding into further and deeper relaxation..."

Indie stared at the hypnotist, who grinned at her and held a finger to her lips but never stopped speaking in that soft tone. Indie realized that the sudden odd comments were probably designed to disorient Kim's mind for a moment, help her let go of the outside world so that she could focus on what was going on inside of her mind. She was amazed, and watched her mother

even more closely.

Kim was completely relaxed by this point, and Indie saw that even the few age lines she had were gone from her face. The doctor spoke softly for a few more moments, and then said, "Kim, I want you to pay attention to me, now. We're going to go back to yesterday and your visit to the dentist. You're in the dentist's office, do you see it?"

"Yes," Kim said. "I'm there."

"Good, now, the dentist is there with you. Tell me what he's saying."

"He says I'm going to be hypnotized so I won't feel any pain, and then he'll give me a shot so it won't hurt later."

"Okay, very good. Now, he's starting the hypnosis process. Tell me what he's saying."

"He's saying I should relax and just listen. He says a lot of things, and then he says I can't feel any pain, and to open my mouth."

"Did he say anything else?"

"He says my cavity is bad, and I should have come in sooner. He's drilling, and he says that he can save my tooth. I can't feel the drill, but I can hear it, and he says he's got to give me a shot so it won't hurt later. I can feel the shot, but it doesn't hurt. He waits a little while and then he's drilling again, and he says the drilling is sort of like sex, and asks me if I like sex, and I say I do, and he says he's going to give me a bottle of medicine and I

should drink it around the middle of the night and come see him, so we can have some great sex."

Dr. Stratton looked alarmed. "And what did he say after that?"

"He says I won't remember that we want to have sex, but I'll wake up around one and drink the bottle, and then I should go to the night club on 18th Street and he'll meet me there and we can have sex. He says he wants to show me what great sex feels like, because he can tell I never had it. He says, no matter what, I shouldn't let anything stop me from getting there, because then I'll never know how good it is."

Dr. Stratton looked at Indie, her eyes wide. "Did it bother you when he said those things?"

"No, I know it should, but it doesn't. I'm just thinking it would be nice to know what great sex feels like."

"And what did he say after that?"

"He says I'm done and I'm going to wake up, and I won't remember anything he told me but I'll wake up at one and drink the bottle and then I'll come to the night club and see him. He says it's time for me to wake up, and I wake up. My mouth is numb from the shot and he says I'm all done and he'll see me next time and then I go out and Indie and I leave. We go to the lab and get my blood drawn again."

"Okay, Kim, when I tell you to wake up, you'll still remember everything he told you, and everything we've talked about today. When I count to three, you'll be

wide-awake and you'll remember everything. One—two—three! Wake up, Kim."

Kim's eyes opened, and she suddenly looked normal. She looked at Dr. Stratton, and then at Indie, and she said, "Oh, that horrible man!" She began to cry, then, and Indie went to put an arm around her.

"He wanted me to go and meet him, I remember now. He said he'd be waiting for me, and I was actually going to go! Oh, dear Lord, why would I do that?"

"Kim," Dr. Stratton said, "it isn't your fault. You couldn't have resisted him. I don't know what was in that shot, but I'm certain it was more than just Novocaine because you should have been able to reject the things he was telling you. Under normal hypnotic induction, you would have been able to, and probably would have awakened and stormed out of there. He was obviously using some sort of drug, and it was probably a dose of the zolpidem. Injected into the tissues of the mouth, it would go straight to the bloodstream in no time flat, and apparently it makes your suggestibility even greater, while eliminating normal inhibitions."

Indie looked at the doctor. "So, that's it? We can prove now that he's doing this?"

The doctor looked at her, and frowned. "Well, unfortunately, this is only one case, and it would be his word against hers as to what really happened in there. I can testify, but his lawyers would get other experts to testify that what I'm saying isn't proven by medical

science, and they'd be right. We need more than just this, but I'm sure it's going to help. I'll write up a report and fax it to the attorney right now."

"What about me?" Kim asked. "Am I out from under him now, or can he still make me do things?"

"In a case like this, his power over you comes from you not realizing that he has it," Dr. Stratton said. "Now that you know, I don't think there's anything else he can do. He probably thinks it didn't work, since you didn't show up last night, and I'm sure that's happened before, so I doubt he'll even try to contact you again, but if he does, you'll be aware and able to resist him."

Indie and Kim left, and drove to Carol's office to let her know what had been learned. By the time they got there, she'd already gotten the doctor's report, and they talked it over for a few minutes.

"I've just gotten a court order for Carl Morris to go to Dr. Stratton today, as well. If she can break through and find out what he was told, then that would be two cases, and with all of the depositions I'm getting today, I think we can get Connors arrested and held, at least, while we work on developing the case. That's what I'm out to do this morning."

They thanked her for working so hard, and then went back to the house. Kim called Grace, Sam's mother, to let her know what they had found out, and Grace was horrified. They talked for a while, and were still talking when Sam called a bit later.

"Hey, baby," he said.

"Hey," Indie replied. "Well, Mom tried to go out in the middle of the night. She took a little bottle out of her purse and tried to drink it, and then she was supposed to go and meet Connors for sex. He'd told her to drink the bottle around one this morning, and that she wasn't to let anything stop her from going to meet him. Sam, that scared me; she was supposed to do anything to get to him, and I would imagine that would even mean hurting someone who tried to stop her! I took the bottle from her and Carol had it analyzed this morning, and it was full of alcohol and zolpidem, so we've got something, at least. Then this morning, I took Mom to a shrink who hypnotized her, and that's how we know what she was told to do."

"Dear God," Sam said. "God, baby, she might have hurt you without even knowing what she was doing!"

"Yeah, but—Sam, it was really weird. She started to drink the bottle, and then she just froze, and she looked at me and said I should take it away from her, but it was like it wasn't her talking, y'know? I asked if she was okay, and she said it wasn't her talking, it was Beauregard, and that Mom was gone in her mind somewhere."

Sam sighed. "Then, for once, I'm thankful she's a split personality nutcase! Beauregard may not be real, but he might have saved your life anyway! Now that we know, though, we've got something. Hopefully, that'll get some attention from the prosecutor, and we may be able

to nail this bastard."

"Carol says it's not enough. She's going to have Carl taken to see the psychiatrist today, too, to see if she can find out what his hypnotic instructions were, and what really happened that night his family was killed. I'm hoping he can handle it, Sam, if it turns out he really did do it."

Sam was quiet for a moment. "We've talked about it," he said, "and Carl knows he probably was the one who was using the tomahawk, but that it wasn't something he would actually do if he were in his own mind. Dr. Connors is the murderer in his case. I don't know what on earth the motive could have been, but somehow, whatever he told Carl to do, it resulted in him killing his family. He knows that, now, and if he can find out what that was, it should be enough to let him live with what happened, I think."

"I hope so," Indie said. "He seems like such a nice man, it's almost impossible to believe he could have done this."

"That's the thing, babe, he couldn't have. But the thing that Connors created by removing all of his inhibitions could, because it wouldn't know any better. Carl wasn't the killer; he was the weapon Connors used to kill those people. I just want to know why, but it could be just that they wanted to stop him from doing whatever it was he was really supposed to do."

"God, this is like a horror movie, like Silence of the

Lambs or something. It's too weird to even comprehend."

"Yeah, it is," Sam said. "Listen, I love you, and Carol is going to be trying to get enough to get me out of here today, so let's hope she can, okay?"

"I love you, too, Sam, and believe me, my fingers are crossed and I'm praying. I think I'm going to ask Anita if Kenzie can just stay down there again tonight; this is too intense, I don't want her to sense everything I'm feeling right now."

"That might be a good idea, sweetheart. If you talk to her, tell her I love her and miss her, okay?"

"I will. Love you!"

"Love you, too, babe. Bye for now."

"Bye."

She had gone into the kitchen when she took the call, so she went back to the living room then, to check on her mother. Kim was sitting upright on the couch, and she had an odd look on her face.

"Mom?" Indie asked. "You okay?"

Kim looked at her and shook her head slowly. "No. Beauregard just told me that there's something bad coming, and that we need to be together for the rest of the day. He says we should be ready to do something terrible, because we may have to, but he won't tell me what it is."

9

Sam and Carl were eating lunch when Carl's name was called. He stuffed the last bite of his bologna sandwich into his mouth and went to where Marilee was waiting at the cellblock door. He spoke to her for a moment, then turned and gave Sam a thumbs-up, before putting his hands behind his back and letting her put cuffs on him.

Sam had told him that Carol was planning to have him taken to a hypnotist, and that he might find out what Connors had done to him, and what had really happened the night his family had died. Carl, who was a religious man, had asked Sam to pray with him, and they'd spent the hour before lunch on their knees together in their cell. Sam had prayed that Carl would be able to cope with what he learned, but Carl had prayed aloud for his family to forgive him for what he'd done, and for God to let them know that it wasn't truly he who

had done it.

Sam had cried with him as they prayed.

With Carl gone from the cellblock, Sam watched the other inmates closely, but none of them seemed inclined to bother him. He went to one of the men and asked to borrow a pen and paper, then sat down at one of the tables and began to write. A new song had begun to form in his head, and he wanted to get it down on paper before he could forget it.

It was a love song to Indie, but it was more than that. His time in prayer had given him a perspective that he hadn't had before, and he wrote a song that not only spoke of his love for her, but of his prayers for God to take care of her, and of her prayers to bring him home.

If only I could hold you in these lonely arms of mine, he wrote,

And shelter you from all the world, and more,

Then I'd be king of all there is, a Monarch in the land,

And you'd be all that I'd be living for,

But as it is, my arms are here, and you're so far from me,

So I bow down each night, and then I pray,

For God to keep you safe for me,

Send comfort in His love,

Until He brings me home to you to stay...

There was more, and he sat there and wrote, praying

as he did so that God would guide the pencil, that this would be the song that would tell Indie how much he loved her, and how much she meant to him. When it was finished, he was amazed that it had come out of him, and then he prayed once more, a prayer of thanks to God for allowing him to write something so beautiful.

* * * * *

Carl was loaded into a van with Detective Kennedy and four officers to escort him to Dr. Stratton's office, though none of them believed for a moment that he would give any resistance. Every officer and jailer who had dealt with him had reached their own conclusion that, somehow, this man was not truly guilty of the crime for which he was incarcerated, and each of them had said their own form of prayer that the truth would come out and that Carl Morris would be able to put this horrible thing behind him.

The ride wasn't long, and the van was taken to a back entrance at the doctor's office, so that people on the street and in her lobby wouldn't stare at Carl. He had two pairs of cuffs on, because of his great physical strength, and his hands were also chained down to his waist. His ankles were linked with shackles, short enough that he could only take baby steps. If he had tried to run, they would have tripped him before he could go ten feet.

Carl wasn't going to run, though. He was on the way to find out what had truly transpired that night, and that was the thing he wanted to know more than anything else

in the world.

He was taken inside through the back door, and then led into Dr. Stratton's office. At her instructions, his restraints were removed, but as they had to, the four guards stood there with their hands on their guns, ready to kill him if he showed any sign of violence. Kennedy stood right beside Carl, but the doctor had the other officers stand as far back against the wall as they could, and then she spoke to Carl.

"Hello, Carl," she said, "I'm Dr. Stratton. What we're planning to do is hypnotize you, and take you back to what happened in Dr. Connors' office last week. After that, we'll go to the night your family was killed, and I'll help you remember what really happened. Are you ready?"

Carl smiled at her. "Yes, Ma'am. I've made my peace with God and my family, but I still need to know what I did, and why I did it."

She smiled back. "I can certainly understand that," she said. "All right, then, let's begin."

She started speaking softly to him, and after a few moments, his eyes slowly closed. Like Kim, his face softened, and within a few minutes, Detective Kennedy thought that Carl looked younger, almost like a child, as the lines of his face smoothed in relaxation. The induction took some time, but after about ten minutes, Carl was fully under and no one there could have doubted it.

"Carl," the doctor said, "I want you to go back to when you went to see the dentist last week. Are you there in the dentist's office?"

"Yes. He had me sit in the dental chair."

"Okay, now, he uses hypnosis, so he's going to hypnotize you. Can you see that happening?"

"Yes. He's telling me to relax, that I won't feel anything. He says I should just listen to him, to everything he says."

"Okay. What does he say after that?"

"He says he's got to give me one shot so my mouth won't hurt later, and that it won't hurt me. I feel it, but it doesn't hurt and then he says he has to wait a few minutes before he can clean my teeth, so he stops talking for a little while."

"And when he starts talking again, what does he say?"

"He says my teeth are in pretty good shape, and then he asks me if I like him, and I say yes, I do. He says if I like him, then I should want to do things for him, and would I do things for him, and I say yes."

Dr. Stratton looked at Kennedy, who was staring at Carl. She held a finger to her lips to remind him to be silent, and he nodded.

"Carl," she said, "what does he say after that?"

"He says he needs me to do him a big favor, and would I do it for him, and I say yes. He says his wife is trying to kill him and he needs me to go and stop her,

but she's so dangerous that the only way I can stop her is to tear her head off, and he asks me if I'm strong enough to do that. I say yes, and he says he's going to give me a bottle of some medicine, and I should drink it around midnight. He says don't let anyone see the bottle and make sure I get rid of it after I drink it. He says I shouldn't let anyone see me drinking it or going to her house, no matter what I have to do, and then I should go to her house and he'll meet me there and let me in. I should go to her bedroom and tear her head off while she's sleeping. He says then he'll let me out and I can go home and go to sleep and I won't remember any of it."

Dr. Stratton had tears in her eyes, but her voice was soft, yet firm. "What does he say after that?"

"He says he's done, and I'm going to wake up and I won't remember what we talked about, but that I'll get up and drink the bottle and then I'll go to her house. He says he knows I know where it is because she works with me sometimes at the Mary Williams home and I've given her rides before."

"And what does he say next?"

"He tells me to wake up and I do, and then I go home."

She stared at him for a moment, shaking her head in disbelief. "Carl, now we're going to that night, and you're in bed sleeping, but suddenly you wake up. You're going to see everything that happened after you woke up, and tell me about it, but you won't get upset, no matter what

happens. Are you there?"

"Yes."

"What do you do when you wake up?"

"I go downstairs and I get the bottle where I put it in my desk, and I drink it."

"And what do you do after that?"

"I go to the door and open it and start to leave, but my son comes out of his room and asks me where I'm going."

"What do you do then?"

"I remember that I'm not supposed to let anyone see me go, and I turn around and go to him and hit him."

The doctor was trembling, and Detective Kennedy was staring in shock. The other deputies were all standing there with their mouths open. "What happens then, Carl?"

"He starts yelling that I'm hurting him, and I hear his mother and sister coming, and I remember that I can't let anyone see or let anything stop me, so I take my tomahawk off the wall where I keep it, and I hit him with it. He falls down and his head is bleeding, but he's trying to get up, so I hit him again with it, and then my wife and daughter are there and they're screaming, so I start hitting them, too. I hit my daughter in the head and she falls down and doesn't move, and my wife is screaming at me and hitting me, so I hit her, too, I hit her in the chest, and I hit her again and again..."

Carl's breath was coming fast, suddenly, as he described what had happened, and he had tears running down his face. "I hit her again and again, and then I hit my daughter again and again and I can't stop, and I hit my son again and again, and I know I need to stop but I can't stop, and then I hear a voice and it says stop, to go and lock the doors and go to sleep, so I stop and I lock all the doors, then I lay down and then I wake up in the jail, and someone told me what I'd done..."

He was becoming agitated. "Carl, relax, that's all over now, just relax. Carl, can you tell me whose voice you heard, who told you to lock the doors and go to sleep?"

Carl was beginning to breathe slower, and he seemed to think about the question for a moment. He leaned his head one way and then the other, and then he said, "I think it was God."

Dr. Stratton looked at Kennedy, but he was obviously shaken. She turned back to Carl, and said, "Okay, Carl, let's come back to today, now. You're going to wake up in a moment, but you're going to remember everything we've talked about. You won't be upset about it, but you'll remember it all. When I count to three, Carl, you're going to wake up. One—two—three."

Carl's eyes slowly opened, as tears continued to fall down his cheeks. He looked at the doctor and smiled. "Thank you," he said.

Kennedy told Sr. Stratton that he wanted a copy of her report, and she promised to send it to him within the

hour. He and the deputies chained Carl again, and led him out to the van. They drove him back to the Detention Center in silence, and shortly he was back in the cellblock with Sam.

He told Sam all of it, and Sam sat in the cell with him as he wept anew.

"Well, that tells us what he really wanted was for you to kill his wife," Sam said, "but by telling you that you couldn't let anyone see you go, he caused the deaths of your family. Carl, I know this is hard on you, but you've got to accept the fact that you were not their killer; Connors was. You were just the weapon he aimed irresponsibly."

Carl nodded. "Yes, I know. I just hope they can bring him to justice, Sam."

"Yeah," Sam said. "Me, too."

* * * * *

Indie had gone down to the Mitchells' house to ask if Kenzie could stay over again, and Anita had assured her it was no problem. "The twins are in heaven," she said, "they're getting all their wildness out! This is good for us, too!"

She told Kenzie that Sam loved and missed her, and promised to give her love to him when she talked to him again, then went back to the house. Her mother was still there, and they sat and talked for a bit, then Kim asked about something to eat. It was well past lunchtime, so she and Indie went into the kitchen and made chicken

noodle soup together.

When they'd eaten, they went back to the living room and found a movie. The two of them sat on the couch, mother and daughter, and laughed their hearts out at Adam Sandler's adventures as a shoe repairman who learns the true meaning of "walking in another man's shoes."

Indie's phone rang at just before 4 p.m., and she looked to see that it was Carol calling.

"Hello?"

"Indie, we're making some serious progress," Carol said. "I've got Will Burton, the deputy prosecutor, ready to sit down and listen to everything in the morning. I tried to get him today, but he's been in court all day and won't give me the time until tomorrow, but we got Carl's hypnosis report today, and it shows that Connors tried to make him kill Mrs. Connors, but—oh, God, it's just too horrific to go into. The poor man did kill his family, but he couldn't possibly have stopped himself."

"Oh, that's awful," Indie said. "But will he be held responsible?"

"Not if I can help it," Carol replied. "I'm out to hang Alex Connors for it, and for his wife's murder, too. The good news is, I'm pretty sure we can get Sam out in the morning, and back to you!"

"Carol, that would be wonderful! Let me know, okay?"

"I will, as soon as I know. Oh, wait! I wanted to tell

you, I talked to Albert Corning a bit ago! He wanted to let me know that his wife is slowly regaining some of her memory, and I got to speak to her doctor and let her know that we've learned about Connors through Carl and your mother, and she said she'd already begun the deprogramming process, based on things Sam told her. Mrs. Corning will probably be able to come home within a few days. I just thought you'd want to know that. Bye!"

She hung up, and Indie let herself breathe a sigh of hope. "That was Carol," she told her mother. "She says the prosecutor is going to look at all of this tomorrow, and there's a good chance Sam will be released. The other man, Carl, it turns out he killed his family, but only because of what Dr. Connors did to him. I don't know the details, yet, but we'll find out tomorrow."

Kim smiled sadly. "When I think that if you hadn't taken precautions, I might have hurt you—Indie, I feel so sorry for that man. I don't know what he's gone through, but I know how I'd feel if I'd done something like that. It would be devastating."

Indie nodded. "I know. If I woke up and found out I'd done something to Kenzie..." She let the thought trail off, because there was nothing suitable to say.

Sam called a little after six. "Hey, babe," she said as she answered. "Have you talked to Carol today?"

"No," he sighed. "She was hoping she might get me out of here today, but I guess it isn't going to happen."

"Well, I talked to her a little while ago, and she said

she's got a meeting with the prosecutor in the morning. She think she's going to be able to convince him to arrest Alex Connors, and drop charges against you, and then she's going after Carl's charges. She wants to have Connors held responsible for that, too, and hopes to get Carl released, and Annie Corning is already showing signs of improvement and getting her memory back."

Sam sighed. "Well, that's something, at least. Carl told me what happened with the hypnotist, and it's helping him, but he still feels some responsibility."

"That's understandable," she said. "It's got to be hard to realize that you did something so terrible, even if you couldn't have kept from it because of something some evil person did to you. I mean, how could you ever accept completely that it wasn't your fault? I know if it was me, I'd be thinking that I should have been strong enough to stop, no matter what had been done to me."

"That's what he's going through, I'm sure. It's just that part of us that thinks we're always in control; when we find out that it's possible for someone else to make us do things so totally against our own natures, it makes us wonder what kind of evil we're capable of on our own. If we're so weak that someone can use a drug to make us do things against our will..."

"I did a little research," Indie said, "and to me, it looks like Connors stumbled across a method of using hypnotic suggestions to actually direct the behaviors of his victims when they're under the influence of the

zolpidem, and since those behaviors are even more intense and uninhibited when alcohol is involved, he figured out that giving them potent alcohol along with it would make them even more likely to do what he wanted them to do. If I were in a college psych class, I'd start writing a paper on it! This is incredibly sinister, but I'd almost bet the government adopts it."

Sam felt a chill. "That's terrifying," he said. "Imagine being able to turn everyday people into assassins or spies, without them even knowing it. I can see Harry Winslow now when he hears about it. 'Hmmm,' he'll say, 'hmmm.' I like Harry, but he's as devious a spy as ever lived, and if he can think of a way to use this to make the country safer, he'd do it."

Indie laughed. "True, but at least he'd only use it for good. Connors was using it to make himself feel like a god, and a man can't get any more evil than that!"

"I know, babe, I know. And speaking of feeling like a god, Carl says that after he killed his family, there was a voice that told him to lock his doors and go to sleep. He says he thought it was the voice of God, but my gut says it was someone a lot more human. I wish there was a way to find out who else could have been there; I'd just about lay odds that Connors was there, somehow, but there's no way to prove it. Carl didn't see whoever was talking to him, so we'll probably never know."

Indie said, "It had to have been whoever called in the tip, Sam. If it was Connors, maybe they can unscramble

the voice and prove it that way. I know there's ways to do that, depending on how it was altered."

"They said they were trying, but hadn't had any luck and weren't sure they could. I'm gonna suggest they check traffic stops, too; sometimes when people are nervous after a crime, they do things that get them stopped, and once in a while, we just get lucky and they get pulled over for a bad taillight or something."

"Sam," Indie said, "Herman can check that—and what about that neighborhood, do they have cameras up on the lights out there? If I could find a picture of Connors' car out there that night, that might help nail him."

Sam smiled into the phone. "Babe, that's brilliant! West Garvin Court, that's in a ritzy neighborhood, and they'd have cameras up because it's a residential area with a lot of kids, and some main streets go through there. You can also check the security companies, see if any of the neighbors use video security. Any camera that could show Connors' car anywhere in that area around that time that night, and the coincidence would be too much to dismiss!"

Indie was excited. She'd been wishing there was something more she could do to help prove the case against Connors was legitimate, and this might be it. What were the odds, she figured, that someone else would have showed up at Carl's house and told him to lock the doors and go to sleep? No one but Connors

would even know he'd respond to such suggestions, and anyone else would surely have screamed and run out the door.

She and Sam said their love words and ended their call, and Indie told her mother what she was going to do, and they went to the office. Kim wasn't very computer literate, so Indie had to explain as she went along.

"Herman, my search bot, can get into just about any database around here, because we've had to do it at one time or another. I'm telling him to check all of the stoplight cameras within two miles of Carl's house between midnight and three AM that morning. He'll get me all of the photos they took, and I can scan through them to see if I can spot Connors' car, which is a..." She looked at a quick report she'd had Herman do for her, and read, "two thousand fifteen Jaguar F-Type Coupe. That's a pretty distinctive car, so it shouldn't be too hard to spot."

She tapped a few more keys. "I'm also telling him to get into all of the local security companies that offer video security, and check to see if any of Carl's neighbors have it. Most people have cameras facing the street, and the video is stored on a server so it can be checked later if necessary. If he finds a house on Carl's street that has it, he'll get me the links to their video storage, too."

Kim watched, fascinated. "The thing I'm wondering," she said, "is how can you tell the police you got this if you do find him? I mean, isn't this illegal without a

warrant?"

Indie smiled. "It would be," she said, "but remember that case where Sam stopped the terrorist? He was granted a Homeland Security Badge and Security Clearance over that, and Harry likes Sam, so he let him keep it. That means that if I find something Sam can use in an investigation, and it turns out we need it to be admissible in court, all we have to do is let Harry know, and he'll arrange a subpoena or a warrant for it. Then I can have Herman generate a report dated after that, and it's good to go."

Kim nodded. "So it's illegal when you do it, but Harry makes it legal to use it, right?"

Indie laughed. "Something like that, yeah." She tapped a few more keys, and Herman got busy. "Okay, this is going to take a couple of hours. Let's go find something to do."

The two of them went back to the living room, and Indie brought a bag of chips and some soft drinks in so they could relax and find a movie. They looked through the list, and found *Maleficent*, which appealed to them both, and decided to watch it.

They enjoyed the movie, and the time together. Indie and her mother had a somewhat tumultuous relationship most of the time, but Kim was a bit subdued after realizing how closely she'd come to trying to harm her daughter, and they were getting along pretty well. Indie was glad, and was enjoying the time while she

could; she was sure it wouldn't last long.

When the movie ended, they went to the office to see how Herman had done. There was a list of cameras on the screen, with hundreds of links that would allow Indie to see what each of them had seen during the time period she had chosen. She clicked the first one, and saw a photo taken at midnight at one of the intersections. There was one car visible, but it wasn't a Jaguar so she went to the next one.

She clicked the link, and looked at another image. This time there were three cars visible, but again, none were Jaguars. She closed it and went to the next.

"We're gonna be at this a while," Kim said, and Indie nodded as she went to the next link.

10

Orville Kennedy was a good cop, and he knew it. He'd been a cop for one force or another for almost thirty years, and his record of arrests was one that was envied by every other cop in Denver County, and probably in the whole state, so he felt justified in feeling that he was good at his job.

Every once in awhile, though, a cop ran across a case that made him feel completely inadequate, and this Carl Morris case had him almost ready to hit the bottle, something he hadn't done in more than ten years. He was sitting in his chair, the one he considered his own chair, the one that was big and worn in and comfortable, and that no one else ever sat in. His wife Jeanie wouldn't sit in it, and when his son Travis had been around, he wouldn't sit in it; it was Orville's, and everyone knew it. It was the chair he sat in when the job was getting to him. He could sit there and let all of the stress sort of leak

out, slowly, and after a few hours, he could put it behind him and let it go.

This case wasn't letting go.

He'd known, the night he'd gone into that house and seen the bloody mess, that there was something not right about it. It wasn't the first time he'd seen a family massacred, not the first time he'd seen it done by a family member and not even the first time he'd found the perp so drunk that he seemed to be in a coma at the scene.

It was, however, the first time he'd seen such a thing after an anonymous tip from someone who took pains not to be identifiable. In crimes like this, anyone who knew enough to call it in was usually crying, screaming, panicking—they weren't under control of themselves enough to take the time to get on a computer or use some smart phone app to disguise their voices. In Orville's experience, the only ones who could do such a thing were people who not only knew about the crime, but were in some manner involved in it. For such a tip to come in meant that there was a person out there who knew that Carl Morris had hacked his family to death, and had done nothing to try to prevent it, done nothing to try to get help before it was too late, and wanted Morris to be seen as the only perpetrator.

Only an accomplice or co-conspirator would want that, and this one fact had troubled Orville ever since he'd walked into that house. Someone knew, but did

nothing to try to save those people.

As he'd done his job and investigated the case, there was nothing to explain that to him, and nothing he found could explain why a well known health nut and teetotaler, a man who was considered a model husband and father who loved his family more than anything, would suddenly get himself dead drunk and take some drugs, then decide in the middle of the night to murder the people who were most important to him in the whole world—and not kill himself in the process.

That was it; when people murdered their families in any way similar to this, they always took their own lives, as well, but Carl hadn't even tried to. From everything they could tell from the crime scene, he had murdered his family, then locked his doors and simply laid down right beside them and passed out cold. The fingerprints on the doors showed that he had blood on his hands when the locks were secured, and that was another odd thing: why weren't the doors secured before the crime? Most people would have locked them first, so that no one could come in and interfere.

These factors bothered Orville, and they had bothered him even before he had gone to the psychiatrist with Carl and his escort that afternoon. He'd heard about the escort just before it was to begin, and since he didn't have anything scheduled at that moment, he decided to ride along and see if any new facts actually came to light. All he'd known was that Carl's lawyer wanted him to be hypnotized to try to learn more about

what had happened that night, and if anything new came out, Orville wanted to hear it. The lawyer hadn't objected to his presence at the interview, so he'd gone along.

He reached into his pocket, took out another cigarette and lit it with trembling fingers. He'd gone along, and he couldn't make up his mind whether he would have done so, if he'd had any idea what he was going to hear.

Carl had done it, from the purely physical standpoint of wielding the weapon and delivering the fatal injuries that claimed the lives of his wife and children. Of that, there was no doubt, and while the report from the psychiatrist could not be considered a confession for the purposes of prosecution, there was no doubt that it detailed precisely what happened during the relatively few moments that were required to bring their lives to their grisly ends. Carl Morris had first struck his son, and when the boy cried out, he had reached for what he knew would be a deadly weapon and used it to kill the boy, and then to kill his daughter and his wife. He had known, at that moment, that he was silencing them permanently, which meant that he was killing them.

However, in the larger sense, Carl hadn't even been there. The man who was Carl Morris had been sent into some dimension where he had no connection to reality, while some creature that had not existed before that morning took control of his body and committed the most horrendous of crimes. Orville, because he'd felt all along that there was something about the case that just

wasn't right, had no problem accepting this fact.

However, the existence of that creature meant that there was a creator that had brought it into existence, and after listening to what he'd heard from Carl under the skilled direction of the hypnotist, he had no doubt that the creator was Alexander Connors.

He'd called Carl's lawyer to ask if there was any other evidence of Connors' culpability, and she had forwarded to him a set of reports and depositions that detailed dozens of arrests that were likely the direct result of Connors' manipulations. The more he read, the more he was appalled and shocked and enraged.

There were cases of women who were apparently "programmed"—he couldn't think of a better word—to meet Connors for sex, and many of the women were quite young. There were people who did incredibly bizarre things after their own treatments by Connors, and many of them had done things that were illegal and dangerous. Some of them had done things so devastating to their own psyches that they had ended up taking their own lives.

Orville had dealt with many evil people throughout his long career, and he had put many of them away in prison, even seen a couple go to death row. Sitting in his chair that night, he couldn't think of one of them who was more deserving of justice than Alex Connors.

The last report he read was from the psychiatrist, and detailed the hypnotic debriefing of a woman who had

actually volunteered to go and see the dentist. She was an attractive woman who did not look her age, according to the report and the attached photos, and Connors had taken the bait. She had been programmed to meet him for sex that night, and might have done so, but her daughter had taken precautions and chained her to a pipe so she couldn't get away. She had also been instructed to make sure no one stopped her from coming, but somehow, the daughter had managed to keep her from hurting herself or anyone else, and the two of them were prepared to testify against Connors if charges could be brought against him.

Orville was worried that the bastard was going to get away with it.

It was terribly hard, he knew, to prove that anyone might be able to cause you to commit a crime by using hypnosis. There had been a few such cases, most of them long ago, but the general consensus today was that a person would not do anything under hypnotic induction that he or she would not do in the waking state.

Orville was convinced that the general consensus would have to be revisited, because there was no doubt in his mind that Connors had found the way to do it. The drug in this case was already known to cause people to do things that were not normal for them, and that normal inhibitions should have prevented, but didn't; by giving people instructions under hypnosis that literally directed the things they would do and the inhibitions

they would ignore, he could actually program them to commit any act he chose. Several of the women who had been his victims, even though they could not prove it at the time, had found themselves involved in sexual practices that left them scarred for life, and some had committed suicide after learning what they had done.

Connors had tried to program Carl Morris to kill his wife, and Orville had no doubt that if he had gotten out without his family seeing him, he almost certainly would have done exactly as he had been told to do—ripped Juliette Connors' head from her body.

Orville picked up the other report he'd gotten from the lawyer, the report on the toxicology scan of the private eye's blood. The drug that was found in his system meant that there was literally no way he could have gone to Mrs. Connors' house and killed her. He would not have been conscious enough to even walk, let alone carry out a complex plot. There was no doubt, based on that report alone, that Sam Prichard was set up, that he'd been carried to that house and left there beside the body, but that someone else had used his gun and fired the shot that killed the woman. Orville considered who could possibly have a motive for wanting Mrs. Connors dead, and the only suspect would be Dr. Connors.

Orville had been a cop for a long time, and one of the things he'd learned was that prosecutors didn't always see things the way cops did. The current prosecutor was one of those that Orville had butted heads with pretty

often, and there were people walking around the streets in the county who, in Orville's opinion, should be serving long prison terms. Some of them had been up on much simpler charges, with far more concrete evidence against them, and yet, because "we might not get a conviction," those charges had been dismissed, or never brought at all.

The lawyer was going to talk to Will Burton, a deputy prosecutor who had some actual *cojones*, but he would have to go to his boss before any charges could be filed. If the only evidence he had to work with was what was in these reports, Orville was afraid the head prosecutor would be afraid of failure and refuse to go after Connors. In order to give Burton what it would take, more evidence was needed, and the most powerful kind of evidence would be a statement by the perpetrator himself.

Orville had faced other such cases, before, where he needed at least a partial confession in order to make the charge stick. He'd gotten confessions, more than once, but he'd been warned that any further confessions that were obtained under the same methods could get him forced into retirement, no matter how well it worked in putting a perp behind bars.

He felt that bringing Alex Connors to justice would be worth being retired. He sat there for a few more minutes and thought that over, made sure that he really felt that way, and then he got up out of his chair and went to the bedroom. Jeanie was sitting up on the bed,

reading as she did most nights. He kissed her and said, "Goin' out for a bit. Got something I need to take care of."

She smiled up at him. "All right, honey," she said. "I'm probably gonna go to sleep, pretty soon."

He smiled back. "I'll try not to wake you when I come in." He kissed her once more and walked out of the bedroom and out of the house. He got into his Ford Expedition and backed out of the driveway.

He knew Connors' address, from all of the things he'd read that day and evening. Each one had contained details of Connors home and office locations, as well as the apartment building he owned, which was where he'd been staying since moving out of the house he had shared with his wife. He drove straight there, expecting to find him at home since it was after eleven.

Sure enough, Connors' Jaguar was in the parking space for his apartment. There weren't any empty spaces, so Orville drove down to the next intersection and turned around, planning to park on the street out front. He had just pulled back onto the street when he saw the Jag's lights come on, and it backed out of its space and started down the street away from him.

Orville followed, using every trick in his long book to avoid being spotted. He let other cars get between them, counting on the Expedition's high stature to let him keep the Jag in view, and switched lanes periodically, just to make things look different in Connors' rear view mirror.

He turned on his low-mounted fog lights once, when Connors turned a corner, then turned them off again at the next turn; all of these tricks were designed to keep a subject from realizing that a single vehicle was staying on his tail.

Connors seemed to have a destination in mind, Orville thought. At one point, when he was only the second car behind him, it looked like the dentist was on his cell phone, but Orville couldn't be sure. He just stayed on the Jag's trail, and waited to find out where the man was headed.

The Jag finally pulled into a parking lot at a bar. Orville thought it was a little odd that a man whose wife had just been murdered would be going out for a drink, but then he remembered that he'd tried to program that PI's mother-in-law to meet him for sex only the day after the murder, so maybe he shouldn't be so surprised.

He parked his car at the edge of the lot, then watched until Connors went inside. When he'd been in for a minute, Orville got out and sauntered toward the door, trying not to be noticeable. He went in, stood near the bar as his eyes adjusted, then scanned the bar in the big mirror until he spotted Connors.

The dentist was sitting near the back wall, at a table by himself. He seemed to be waiting for someone, and when a young woman entered a few moments later and immediately sat down at his table, he suspected that he was witnessing the beginning of one of Connors' drug-

fueled rapes.

The girl seemed enchanted by Connors, smiling and reaching out to touch him. She didn't object when he grabbed her by her hair and pulled her into a kiss, and when it became obvious that he was touching her breast, she only giggled happily. Orville guessed the girl at being in her late teens or really early twenties, and just watching was making him angry and sickened.

Orville couldn't let it go on. He rose from where he'd been nursing a Coke at the bar, and walked straight to Connors' table and sat down opposite him.

Connors looked at him, surprised. "Is there something I can do for you?" he asked.

Orville nodded, and then took out his shield case and held it so Connors could see it. "Yeah, you can let this little girl go home."

Connors smiled. He turned to the girl and asked, "Penny, do you want to go home?"

Penny laughed, a sultry laugh that shouldn't come from one so young. "Huh-uh, I wanna have fun! Let's go have fun!" She had her arms around Connors' neck, and was acting like a lovesick schoolgirl.

Orville leaned forward. "Look, you sick son-of-a-bitch," he said. "Your game's over. We know it all, now, Connors, all about how you program people to do what you want with your hypnotism and the drugs you use, and we've got all the evidence we need. Tomorrow sometime, you're gonna be arrested, and when the

Grand Jury gets done indicting you, I figure you're looking at a few hundred years in prison. Send the girl on her way, and then go home and stay there till we come for you."

Connors stared at him, and Orville could see the man's mind racing like made. He started to speak a couple of times, but closed his mouth, and then it looked like some kind of resignation came over his face, like he was accepting that something he'd dreaded had finally come true.

"How?" he asked. "I've always covered my tracks. How did you figure it out?"

Orville snorted. "We didn't," he said. "Some private eye did, and then his wife and her momma set you up for the big fall! Remember that little hottie you tried to set up for last night? She was the PI's mother-in-law, and they got her blood samples to prove you doped her up. And that little bottle of happy juice you gave her? Well, they tested that, too, and your ass is cooked once the prosecutor sees it all tomorrow morning."

Connors stared at him. "They set me up?" he asked, incredulous. "They actually tried to set me up? How did they keep her from coming to me last night, did they keep her locked up all night?"

"Her daughter did, yeah, and then today they went to a real hypnotist, and got everything out of her. How she was supposed to meet you for sex, how she wasn't supposed to let anything stop her. And guess what they

did after that? They got Carl Morris out of his cell, and took him down to that same doctor, and he told them all about how you wanted him to kill your wife, and how you told him not to let anyone know what he was doing. You son of a bitch, you made that poor man kill his own wife and kids with that crap, and if it's the last thing I ever do, I'm gonna see that you go down for that, instead of him!"

Connors sighed, and pinched the bridge of his nose. "Do you really think it's that easy?" he asked. "Do you really think I wouldn't have plans for when this might happen?" He turned to the girl. "Penny, this man is trying to rape you, and you don't want that. You need to scream for help."

Penny leapt from her chair, and before Orville could react, she began to scream. "Help!" she screamed, pointing at Orville, "Help, he's trying to rape me! Help!"

A half-dozen men grabbed at Orville, and nobody even heard him trying to identify himself as a cop. He was thrown to the floor, and he heard Connors yell that someone should call the police, and he turned his head to look at the dentist, just in time to see him hand something to Penny and whisper into her ear. She nodded, and looked at Orville with a rage in her face, and then she screamed and launched herself at him, her hand raised, and Orville saw the long knife in her hand as she brought it down into his chest. The men who were

holding him began to scream, then, but the knife went up and down, over and over, and the last thing Orville Kennedy saw before the blackness descended was that Connors was no longer there.

* * * * *

Connors wasn't as surprised as Orville had thought he would be. When you've created a way to become like a god on earth, there will always be those who want to destroy you, who want to stop you, and he knew that. It had been the same way back in college twenty years ago, when he'd first begun developing his techniques. He'd been given Adivol by a friend, who said it was awesome at making girls more cooperative, and when he'd seen just how effective it was in turning normally prudish girls, even the Jesus-freak girls, into raving nymphomaniacs, he realized that it had some sort of inhibition-deactivation effect. That had prompted him to do some research, which he originally planned to lead to his doctoral dissertation in psychology; however, his dissertation adviser had pushed him to move into other areas, and since his adviser was chair of the dissertation committee, he had decided to do as he was told.

His decision to go into dentistry had been fueled, in part, by his research. He wanted to go into a field that would allow him access to patients who would be amenable to both hypnosis and medication, and when an audited seminar on hypnosis promoted it as a leading form of anesthesia in dentistry, he'd been sold! That only required him to find ways to get the initial dose of Adivol

into them, and he solved that by adding it to the Novocaine that he injected into the gums. By injecting it into the mouth, the zolpidem solution went almost instantly to the bloodstream.

Since the patient was already under hypnotic induction, he could bypass the sleep inducing function of the drug, and the patient would remain awake, though some of them seemed drowsy. They always blamed that on the effects of the Novocaine itself, so it never caused a problem. For almost twenty years, he'd used this technique to seduce the most beautiful women, milk wealthy clients for millions of dollars in fees for services they believed he'd rendered, though he often hadn't, and he'd even developed his techniques to the point that he could make people do literally anything he wanted them to do.

His first experiments with that had been incredible; he'd been attacked and beaten by a man who had followed his wife and found her meeting Connors at a motel room. He'd been enraged, but he was no match, physically, for his attacker, and so he seethed for weeks, planning an appropriate revenge.

The man ran a construction company, and had several projects going around the area, and Connors made it his business to learn all he could about them. His opportunity came almost two months later, when a man who worked with the attacker came in for a root canal. Connors had given him the drug, and carefully programmed him to take the additional dose the

following morning at work, then follow his boss up onto the roof of the eight-story building they were working on. The attacker fell to his death, and there were apparently no witnesses.

Connors had realized then that he was almost a god and that he could do anything and get away with it. He had stepped up his experiments, then, adding in other things that he knew would increase his feeling of omnipotence. When a friend had come to him complaining that his business partner was about to reveal some things he had done that would probably lead to jail time, Connors programmed an older patient to go and shoot the partner dead. The killer was caught, sleeping in his car just outside the scene of the crime, and swore that he had no idea what had happened. Police could find no connection between the two, and when a psychiatrist had testified that the man honestly had no memory of what had happened, it had resulted in the killer being sent to a mental institution instead of standing trial.

Connors was invincible. He could eliminate any problem for anyone, and it wasn't long before he let a few trusted people know that he could do so. Over the past ten years, he had caused witnesses to disappear completely, made evidence vanish, and arranged for certain women to suddenly find a man who desired them irresistible. His fees were high, but he almost always delivered.

Sure, there were occasional problems, but he took

care of them. When a couple of the women he'd chosen for himself woke up too soon and realized they were in bed with him, they had protested and even accused him of somehow forcing them, but that was why he always met them in public places. Witnesses and security tapes would show that they were not only willing to leave with him, but insistent. When they realized that, they dropped everything, and all he'd had to do was use his talents to make his wife let it go.

Juliette had been one of his most successful experiments. Beautiful, young and fairly rich, she had married him while he was still in college working on his psych degree, and then she had paid for his dental schooling. She had been one of the girls he had programmed to date him back in school, but when her money had come to light, he had continued programming her every time they met until she was certain that she was in love with him. Her family had never understood why she chose him, but once they were married, they had accepted him.

Unfortunately, she had slowly become less susceptible to his control. After the first few times he was caught with other women, she had stopped being as forgiving as he'd liked, and eventually they began to fight over his affairs. For a long time, she had almost ignored him, and it finally hit him that it was because he was finally wealthier than she was; that was when he began setting up his offshore accounts. He pretended to be a tax protester, but the truth was that he always paid the

taxes on his income, then hid it so she couldn't get to it.

He'd known that divorce would be coming sooner or later, and he'd even thought more than once of just having her killed—but he actually did care for her, at least enough to avoid murdering her until it became necessary. When she started asking questions about his hidden accounts, it had been the last straw, and he'd planned it out carefully. He chose a patient who had already done some minor things for him, a strong and powerful man who could kill her quickly and easily. Carl Morris was a fairly simple man, and he took his programming easily.

Connors was so excited about getting Juliette out of the way that he decided to take a risk and go and watch. He'd gone to Carl's house, planning to follow him and make sure there weren't any complications, but there had been. He'd been parked just in front of the house next door, and he saw the front door start to open—but then it closed, and he'd wondered what was going on. He'd stepped out of his car, and that was when he heard the first scream.

He rushed to the door and found it half open, so he's pushed it a bit further to see if he could tell what was going on. Carl had his son down on the floor, and as Connors watched, he struck the boy in the head with a hatchet or something. A second later, a woman and a girl came running in and grabbed him, trying to stop him, but he struck them both savagely, hitting them over and over until they both were motionless and silent. He

started to rise, and Connors knew that, in this condition, Carl would leave a trail a mile wide, even if he managed not to get stopped on the way to Juliette's place, so he decided to abort the plan.

He said, "Carl, stop. I want you to forget what you were supposed to do, and go and lock your doors, then lay down and go back to sleep. Lock your doors, Carl, and then go back to sleep, do you understand?"

Carl had not even looked his way. He nodded and said, "I'll lock the doors, then go to sleep," and turned to shuffle to the front door. Connors backed away, and when he heard the door latch click shut, and then the deadbolts slide home, he turned and sprinted hurriedly to his car and went straight home.

He was trembling, but it wasn't with fear or remorse; he had just witnessed exactly how powerful he really was, and seeing those people die so violently had left him in a heightened state of excitement that he'd never known before. He got to his apartment and rushed inside, locking the door behind him and then sitting in a chair the rest of the night, reliving the experience over and over.

It was almost like he'd killed those people himself, but that was thrill he'd never known. He'd dreamed about it, but he'd always felt that it would be senseless to take any of the risks upon himself, so he had never allowed himself to act on it.

Then that stupid PI had showed up at his office, and

he'd gotten angry. He knew it was the same one that had done the asset search his lawyer had faxed to him that morning, but he pretended to know nothing. When it dawned on him that this young punk actually knew what he was doing, what he was capable of, it had infuriated him. He needed a way to get rid of him, and suddenly it hit him that he could use the PI to his advantage.

When Sam had stood to go, Connors had risen behind him, and driven a hypodermic needle full of ketamine—one he kept prepared at all times—into his lower back. Sam had spun, of course, and tried to put up a fight, but the proximity to the kidneys had meant that the drug was in his bloodstream within seconds. Sam's bad hip had worked against him, and he'd fallen as he spun, and by the time he was able to start getting to his feet, he was so woozy and weak that he couldn't manage it, and a moment later he was out cold.

Connors had called for Gina, his hygienist and Becky, the receptionist, the two women who were his greatest successes. Both of them took daily reinforcements of his programming, and would automatically do anything he told them to do. He told the receptionist to tell anyone who came in that he was indisposed in the bathroom, and then had the hygienist help him carry Sam out to his car.

He spotted Sam's motorcycle, and called a friend who owed him a big favor. The motorcycle would be gone within minutes, and would cease to exist in only a few hours.

They drove straight to Juliette's house, and Connors had taken Sam's gun and gone to ring the doorbell. When Juliette answered the door, her face set in a smirk, it had pissed him off even more, and he'd raised the gun and pointed it into her face. She'd stumbled back, begging him not to do anything stupid, and suddenly he'd just had his fill, of her, of wanting to feel the thrill of a kill, of being *almost*—but not quite—omnipotent, and he'd pointed the gun and pulled the trigger, firing once, twice, a third time...

The first bullet had caught her just over the right eye, and she was dead instantly, her brain gone and splattered all over the wall behind her. The second bullet had struck her right shoulder, and the third had gone wild, burying itself in a bookcase. He'd stood there staring at what he'd done for a moment, and then the thrill hit him so hard that he had an orgasm.

He'd gone to the car, and he and the hygienist had carried Sam in. They laid him down next to Juliette's body, and Sam told Gina to rub Sam's hand in the blood that was all over the floor and then wrap it around the grips of the gun and use his finger to fire one more shot. That would put powder residue on Sam's hand, Connors knew, and that would be important.

Then they'd gone back to the office, Gina keeping her bloodied hand up so that she wouldn't risk leaving any blood spots in the Jag. When they'd gotten back, the receptionist said no one had come in, so he told her to make sure that no one ever knew he had left that day.

Both she and Gina were programmed to believe that they had seen Sam leave angrily. Gina washed up, and then forgot the entire episode as she was told to, and Connors composed himself and got ready for the visit from the police that was sure to come.

A half hour later, it dawned on him that Sam would be waking up soon, and he needed the police to find him there with the body. He called Gina in and told her to go to the convenience store that was only a few blocks from Juliette's place and use the payphone there to call the police and report hearing shots from the house. She was to refuse to give a name, and then get back as soon as possible. She did as she was told, promptly forgot it, and was back almost an hour before the police showed up to tell him his wife had been murdered.

But all of it was falling apart on him. That stupid PI and his wife and her mother had ruined everything! Well, the PI was in jail, and he couldn't get to him; all that remained was to deal with the wife and mother!

11

Indie and Kim had been at the computer for hours. They'd looked at more than three hundred images, and were just about ready to conclude that Connors hadn't been near Carl's house the night of the murder, but commitment and loyalty to Sam made them keep looking. Indie saw that it was almost 2 a.m., and she knew they were both exhausted, but she didn't want to quit. If they could find one image of Connors' Jaguar anywhere in that area that night, it should be enough to make a jury believe he could have been in Carl's house that night. Every little thing they got on Connors would help when it came time for the prosecutor to make his decision on Sam, as well as on Carl. She kept going.

She clicked another link, and they looked at the cars in the picture. "Nope," Kim said, and she closed that window. She clicked the next, with the same result. Kim yawned beside her as she clicked the next one, and said,

"Nope," as she yawned, but Indie said, "Wait!"

She looked closely at the image on the screen, and then went to another window where she had a picture of a Jag like Connors' saved for comparison. She went back and forth a few times, and then Kim said, "Holy mother, you got him!"

"Yeah, I think so. Now, let's get the tag from that car," she said, blowing up the image and moving it so they could see the license plate on the front of the car. "AQR 912," she said, then looked at a note on her desk.

Kim jumped out of her chair when Indie slapped her desk and shouted, "*Bingo!* We've got him! That's his car, right there, and if you take a good look, I'll bet you can recognize your old friend the dentist, there!"

Kim leaned close to the screen and looked closely at the blown-up image. "That's him. I'd know that shiny bald head anywhere, now!"

"Do you mean this shiny bald head?" said a voice behind them, and both Indie and Kim turned to find Alex Connors standing behind them. He had a chrome-plated automatic in his right hand, and it was waving back and forth between them. "Well, hello, Kimberly. Since you remember me so well, I must have made quite an impression on you. Why didn't you introduce me to your daughter, yesterday? Why, the three of us could have had so much fun together!" He sighed. "But you had to play detective, and try to ruin everything for me, didn't you? Well, I guess I can understand; it was your

move, I suppose, but what you need to understand is that you're playing against a master, and I never lose."

Indie stared at him and his gun, trying to think of anything she could say or do to save their lives, but she was at a loss. She couldn't understand how he could have gotten in, she was sure she'd locked the door, but that wasn't important; he was there, and he apparently planned to kill them both. The only thing she could think of was to thank God that Kenzie wasn't home, because this sick monster would have killed her, too. She knew that Sam would do his best to raise the child, and that he'd make sure she didn't forget her mother.

"If you hurt us, the police will know who did it," she said, and then kicked herself mentally. This was a man who thought he was above the law, and beyond the reach of justice. That was obvious, from everything he had done so far. His delusions of grandeur and invincibility blinded him to the mistakes he'd made, and he wouldn't believe anything she said about getting caught.

"Oh, I've already dealt with one of them," he said, "and I had planned for this contingency a long time ago. I'll be long gone before your bodies are found, with a new name and no way I can be found, so I'm not concerned about any repercussions. But I do want to know one thing, before I do what I came to do, and that's how you did all this. How did you and your husband figure me out?"

Indie thought fast; he was giving her a chance to buy

time, as stupid as any movie villain. If she could use it properly, there was a slim chance she could get some kind of advantage, and she prayed she'd know it if she saw it.

"I'm a computer whiz," she said slowly. "I was looking at your business records, and checked your patient logs, and saw that Carl Morris was one of your patients, and that he'd been there the morning before he killed his family, and then I saw that Annie Corning was there before she started acting strange, and I put two and two together and got four. There were too many coincidences."

Connors smiled. "Wow, what a smart girl you are," he said. "Still, there was nothing to connect me to them. How did you get that cop to believe you?"

Indie didn't know what cop he could be talking about, because as far as she knew, none of the police involved would know anything about it until after Carol met with the prosecutor in the morning. She didn't want to lose the advantage, though, so she shrugged as it was no big deal.

"I just showed 'em everything I had, and they came to their own conclusions," she said.

Kim leaned forward suddenly, smiling. "And that's why they said you might come after us," she said, "and put officers to watching the house from hiding. Between that and the video cameras we hid all over the place, we've got an audience of about twenty people watching

us right now."

Connors' face went blank, and his eyes began flashing around the room. "What cameras? I don't see any cameras..."

Indie seized on her mom's idea. "We use nanny cams, heard of those? See the clock on the wall? Camera. See the plant over there on the desk? Camera. There are about twenty scattered around here, and I suspect our guard detail will be coming through the doors any second now!"

Connors stared at her, but his eyes kept flicking to the clock and the plant, then back to her face. He stood there for a moment in shock, but then his face contorted in rage.

"*No!*" he screamed, "no!" He had lowered the gun slightly, letting its aim hang down toward the desk for a second, but he suddenly started to raise it, and then he froze again. Indie stared at him for a second, and then realized that his eyes weren't on her any longer, they were looking to her right, and there was blood on his chest. Indie turned her head to her right, and saw her mother standing there with Sam's other gun, the little thirty-two with the silencer that Harry had given him when he was dealing with the terrorist.

Connors fell to the floor, and Indie immediately jumped up and grabbed his gun from him as he hit. She felt for a pulse and found one, weak but somewhat steady, and then grabbed the phone to dial 911.

"I need police and an ambulance right now," she said, then looked at her mother's face. "I've just shot an intruder who was trying to kill me and my mother. No, he's down and wounded, but alive. Yes, we'll have the front door open."

She got off the phone and turned to look at her mother. "Mom? Mom, give me the gun..."

"I shot him," Kim said slowly. "Beauregard said I would have to do something terrible, but I didn't know I'd have to shoot him..."

Indie reached out and took the gun, slowly and carefully, and her mother turned to look at her. "Mom, it's okay," she said. "You saved our lives, Mom, it's okay."

Kim stared at her for a moment. "Beauregard told me the gun was in the desk drawer, and to open the drawer while we were looking at the computer. When he lowered his gun, he told me to get it and shoot him, and I did..."

Indie swallowed. "Okay, and you did, you saved our lives, but I think—I think when the cops get here, it would be better if we say I shot him, okay? And let's—let's just leave Beauregard out of it completely, shall we?"

* * * * *

Karen Parks was called out of a dead sleep to respond when the call came in that Orville Kennedy had been stabbed numerous times at a bar on Eighteenth Street. When she arrived, she found that he was badly

injured, but alive, and left her assistant Brenner to get witness statements and handle the perp—a young girl who swore she didn't remember doing it—while she went with Kennedy to the hospital.

He regained consciousness in the ER, and was able to tell Karen how he'd come to be at the bar, and why. She had not yet been briefed on Connors, and was having a hard time believing what she was hearing, but she knew Orville; if he said it, she believed it. When she heard that there was even evidence that Sam Prichard was innocent, she breathed a sigh of relief, because she owed that man.

She was still there, waiting with Jeanie for him to get out of emergency surgery, when the next call came in two hours later, that Sam Prichard's wife had just shot an intruder, so she left and threw her light on the dash as she raced to Sam's place.

The intruder was none other than Alex Connors himself. Karen had let the paramedics work on him, then took Indie and Kim to the station to be interviewed. By the time they had all of the reports and statements— with some strange comment about someone named Beauregard, which Indie insisted was a delusion of her mother's, brought on by the shock of the whole situation —and knew what had actually happened, it was almost 10 a.m., and Karen was surprised when she got a call from the prosecutor's office. She slipped out of the room to take it.

"Parks," she answered.

"Karen," said a tired voice, "this is Will Burton. I've been going over an absolutely humongous pile of science fiction that happens to be highly detailed and uncannily credible evidence that we have a man in this city who has literally been using mind control to make people commit murder and other crimes."

"Yes, sir," she said. "I'm dealing with part of that situation right now. Alex Connors attempted to kill two people early this morning, and got himself shot in the process. It's not a life-threatening wound, and he's in custody at the hospital now. I'm going over it all with the wife of Sam Prichard, the private investigator; it was her and her mother that Connors tried to kill, and the wife who shot him."

Burton sighed. "And she didn't have the decency to finish the job for us? Tell her I hate her. Anyway—I've seen enough to say that Prichard is almost certainly innocent, and I can guarantee we'd never get a conviction against him in any event, so I've just sent a motion to the judge to dismiss, and it's been granted already. He'll be released any second now, so you're off that case."

Karen smiled. "I'm glad to hear it, and I'll share the news with his wife. Any word on the Carl Morris case? I hear it's right in the middle of this mess."

"Oh, dear God, Karen, do you know who my boss is? When I told him there is evidence that Morris was manipulated beyond any hope of resistance into doing

that deed, he threw a fit at first. It took us an hour to convince him he isn't going to get a conviction, but that wasn't good enough for him. He's decided to offer Morris a deal: no jail time, if he pleads to manslaughter and agrees to testify against Connors. His lawyer called me ten minutes ago to say he accepted, so we're going to court to close the deal this afternoon."

Karen thanked him and hung up the phone, then went to tell Indie the good news.

* * * * *

Sam and Indie arrived at the Casino an hour before the band was scheduled to play. Because they were playing in the lounge and alcohol would be served, minors weren't allowed, and Kenzie was happily staying with the twins again that night. They went inside and found the seats they'd asked for, reserved for Indie, their mothers and a couple of guests: Harry Winslow and Carl Morris. Carl had been released the day after Sam; he'd accepted the plea agreement, pleading guilty to manslaughter in return for one year of probation and psychological counseling. Sam had invited him to attend the show, and he'd been happy to accept, once he got over the shock of his private investigator being a performing country singer.

Once they were all there and seated—Grace, Sam's mother, had Harry parked right beside her, and Kim was doing her best to provide friendly conversation to Carl—Sam went back to get changed and ready.

Chris spotted him first. "Sam, good deal!" he called out. "We're all set, are you?"

"Yep," he said. "Let's do it now, we don't have a lot of time." He pulled printed sheets out of a pocket and passed them around, then took the acoustic guitar Chris handed him, strummed it a couple of times, and then began to sing. The rest of them listened, making notes on paper that would be meaningless to anyone else, but to them was a chart that would become music as soon as they got on stage.

"Okay," Sam said. "What do you guys think?"

Candy threw her arms around his neck and hugged him, tears in her eyes. "Sam, that's one of your best yet! Indie's gonna be blown away. Are you sure she doesn't know anything about it?"

Sam grinned. "Nothing at all! I wrote it while I was in jail, memorized it and gave the original to Carl to hold for me. He's got it, and he'll give it to her when we do the song on stage."

They had Sam go through it once more, so they were all sure they had their parts figured out, and then it was time to get on the stage and get ready. The lights were off, and no one could actually see them as they got into place and prepared for the moment of truth.

The lights came on, and the announcer's voice said, "Everyone, put your hands together and give a big Casino welcome to our newest act—*Step—Back—Once!*"

Chris lit up his guitar with the opening riffs of *I Got*

Married In The Elvis Room Last Night, and the crowd got into it almost instantly. When Sam started singing, they began dancing in their seats, and by the time he hit the third line, the dance floor was filling up.

They went through *No Happy Endings,* and Sam was surprised to see quite a few people dancing to that one, as well, some of them getting so creative that he was amazed even as he sang. He let the final notes roll off, and then Sam signaled the light man, and a spotlight hit Indie.

"Ladies and gentlemen," he said, "I'm Sam Prichard, lead singer and chief songwriter for Step Back Once, and that beautiful young lady right there is my wife, Indiana. She is the inspiration for all of the love songs I write, and now and then I like to surprise her with a new one. Tonight, you all get to help me do that, because the song you're about to hear has never been performed in public before." He looked down at Indie and blew her a kiss. "This is for you, babe," he said, and then Chris began to play.

If only I could hold you in these lonely arms of mine,

And shelter you from all the world, and more,

Then I'd be king of all there is, a Monarch in the land,

And you'd be all that I'd be living for,

But as it is, my arms are here, and you're so far from me,

So I bow down each night, and then I pray,
For God to keep you safe for me,
Send comfort in His love,
Until He brings me home to you to stay...

And somewhere up in Heaven,
There's an angel just for me,
God put him there to do what I can't do,
His name means, "Love, Forever,"
His robe will dry your eyes,
His wings will always fly my love to you...
Whenever you remember, all those times I held you near,
That's when he dries the lonely tears you've cried,
And when you're softly sleeping, in some sweet dream of me,
He's whisp'ring all the love I feel inside,
And when you sit there cryin', and pray for my return,
And ask the Lord to let me soon be there,
The angel flies to Hea-ea-ven and kneels before the Throne,
To lay before the Lord your loving prayer,

And somewhere up in Heaven,

An angel sheds a tear,

As God looks down with love on you and me,

And shakes his head in wonder,

That we made an angel cry,

For an angel's tears were never meant to be

And somewhere up in Heaven,

An angel sheds a tear,

As God looks down with love on you and me,

And shakes his head in wonder,

That we made an angel cry,

For an angel's tears were never meant to be

No, an angel's tears were never meant to be

Indie sat there in tears as the final strains died away, and the crowd went wild. A dozen people ran over to shake Indie's hand, and twice as many ran up to tell Sam how much they loved the song. It took a few moments for everything to settle down, and the show went on.

When the show was over, Sam flopped into a chair beside Indie and ordered a cold soft drink. When the barmaid brought it back, she handed him an envelope and said, "There's a guy out back who gave this to one of the bouncers and asked to see that it got to you."

Sam took it and looked at it, then opened it up. Inside were three photographs and a sheet of paper.

When he took them out, he saw that the photos were of three different people, two women and one man, whose faces had been obscured. He unfolded the sheet of paper and saw that it was typed, probably from a cheap, throwaway printer. He read through it once, then passed it to Indie.

"*Mr. Prichard,*" it said, "*the people you see in the photos will be killed within the next forty-eight hours, unless you stop me. I have been following your exploits closely, and I think that you are the one I need to make sure I stop doing this. I've been trying for more than fifteen years to kick this habit, but I can't.*

Normally, I don't strike so many times so close together, but in order to get you interested, I'm going to up the odds. I need you to do only two things: discover who each of my victims are, and then do all you can to stop me before I can kill each one. The first one will die exactly twenty-four hours after you receive this note; the second will die twelve hours after that, and the third twelve hours later. If you cannot stop me before I can kill the third one, then no one can. Then there will be a fourth victim, but you get no clues for that one."

Indie read it two times, and then passed it to Harry. "Sam?" she said. "Any idea who sent it to you?"

Sam shook his head. "Not even a clue."

Harry read it quickly, and passed it back to Sam. "What do you plan to do, son?" he asked.

Sam shrugged. "I guess I'm gonna find a killer. Indie

and I will get started as soon as we get home."

BOOK 5
THE KILL LIST

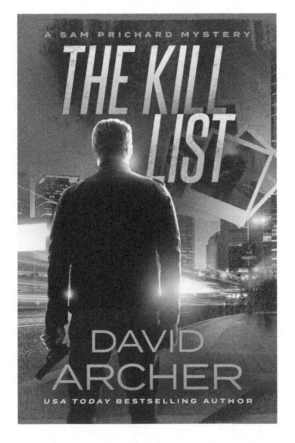

AVAILABLE ON AMAZON

ABOUT

David Archer was born and raised in Bakersfield, California. He is a fiction author and novelist, writing in the mysteries and thrillers genre. His approach to writing is to hit deep, keep you entertained, and leave you wanting MORE with every turn of the page. He writes mysteries, thrillers, and suspense novels, all of which are primed to get your heart pumping.

The author's books are a mixture of mystery, action, suspense, and humor. If you're looking for a good place to start, take a look at his bestselling Sam Prichard Novels, available now. You can grab copies in eBook, Audio, or Paperback on all major retailers.

Made in United States
North Haven, CT
18 June 2023

37899037R00129

Framed

Published by: David Archer

USA TODAY BESTSELLING AUTHOR

DAVID ARCHER

FRAMED

A SAM PRICHARD MYSTERY

FRAMED